SHERLOCK HOLMES &
THE CHILFORD RIPPER

Sherlock Holmes & The Chilford Ripper

by

Roger Jaynes

Dales Large Print Books
Long Preston, North Yorkshire,
BD23 4ND, England.

British Library Cataloguing in Publication Data.

Jaynes, Roger
    Sherlock Holmes & the Chilford ripper.

    A catalogue record of this book is
    available from the British Library

    ISBN   978-1-84262-546-0 pbk

First published in Great Britain in 2006
by The Irregular Special Press for Baker Street Studios Ltd
under the Breese Books Imprint

Published in Large Print 2007 by arrangement with
Baker Street Studios Ltd.

Dales Large Print is an imprint of Library Magna Books Ltd.

Printed and bound in Great Britain by
T.J. (International) Ltd., Cornwall, PL28 8RW

To my Mary, with love

'My life is spent in one long effort to escape from the commonplaces of existence. These little problems help me to do so.'

Sherlock Holmes,
The Red-Headed League

Watson's Foreword:

A request and an affirmation

Not long after Sherlock Holmes' retirement, I received an unexpected letter from J. Thurgood Morton, a representative of my longtime publisher, *The Strand Magazine*, inquiring as to whether or not I planned to chronicle more of my illustrious friend's adventures, and if so, when?

Given the volume of correspondence that had crossed his desk in recent months, he wrote, it was strikingly clear that the public was still quite eager to, as he put it, 'take up the chase' and read more of Holmes' intriguing and singular exploits. Surely, he insisted, there must be at least a few more cases of interest that I might recall, and would be willing to set forth in print. If this were so, he assured me that *The Strand Magazine* would publish any and all, and that the financial terms would certainly be to my liking. His hope, he concluded, was that a new Holmes story might appear in the very next issue, but that deadlines were fast approaching. He requested that I reply – a little too eagerly, I felt – at my earliest convenience.

I would be far from honest if I did not admit that that his letter, even though it contained many flattering comments concerning my literary talents, was an unwelcome intrusion into what had become for me a relatively quiet and peaceful existence since Holmes' departure from London to become a keeper of bees in Sussex. I, soon after, had also left our rooms at Baker Street, and had remarried again the following spring. My practice, at this time, was quite successful, though not so burdensome that it proved to be a strain. In addition, my new wife was undeniably happy that Holmes now seemed safely tucked away amidst his books and bees on the South Downs. (I must admit, the first months of our marriage had teetered on disaster, when Holmes, unable at first to give up the game, had twice suddenly appeared on our doorstep, asking that I find my service revolver and accompany him into the night, hot on the scent of a case that he had only just accepted. This, it turned out, was more than my other half's fragile nature could handle, and so, after the second incident, she made me promise there would be no more such nocturnal excursions. Ah, if she had only been more like my Mary...)

What Morton did not realise, of course, was that the problem in setting down more of Holmes' sundry and bizarre adventures was never a lack of material, but rather what should, or should not, be revealed to the public. My bulging files all but overflowed with my meticulous handwritten notebooks, chronicling the details of more than a hundred still unrevealed cases that had come our way during the years we shared rooms together. Some, while an admirable test for my companion's remarkable powers of observation and deduction, were frankly, I felt, rather mundane affairs of small consequence that I adjudged to be of little general interest. Others, especially those requests handled on behalf of the Royal Family or Holmes' brother Mycroft, not to mention a half dozen dignitaries from other Continental powers, were still far too sensitive to see public light.

Another formidable barrier was Holmes himself. He had, after all, raised on more than one occasion objections to the manner in which I chronicled his experiences in crime. So it was with apprehension that I now wrote to him, asking his permission and advice as to which unpublished cases, solved during our long association together, he would consent to my putting on paper. To publish without doing so would be an indiscretion I could never commit.

When a fortnight passed without reply, my anxieties mounted. Some days later, my hand fairly trembled, as I plucked from the letters upon my desk an envelope bearing an Eastbourne postmark and addressed in what I immediately recognised as Holmes' unmistakable hand. For better or worse, I felt, there was no sense in delaying the inevitable, and hurriedly ripped the missive open.

Imagine then, my delight when I read:

Good old Watson!
You always were the soul of discretion, and I am deeply touched that even now you would first consult me before writing of events long past. Based on your recent accounts of our earlier dealings with the late Professor Moriarty, I now see that my previous fears of damaging publicity were quite unfounded. From this day, I say, write what you will, my faithful Boswell. You have remained a trustworthy and loyal friend, and in matters of this sort I will hereafter trust your judgement completely.

Why not reveal, for example, the details of our unexpected trip to Chilford in the autumn of '94 – that gruesome affair that took place at the end of our uneventful summer following the capture of Colonel Moran. I cannot imagine that it would now do any harm. A decade has passed since we went to the aid of your friend Geoffrey Blake.

You might also consider the case of Colonel Collingwood's niece, as you chose to call it at the time (if she is not living still in England), though a few aliases would most certainly be in order to protect her unknowing relatives. To have flushed out the murderer because of his love of Japanese oysters was, I admit, no easy feat. And then, of course there was the Wilcox matter, another gruesome business, and certainly not without its lurid points of interest.

I think for now, dear Watson, these should suffice, though I stress again that I now leave to your judgement which of those many intriguing, and oft-times dangerous adventures we undertook should see the light of day. I can only thank you once again for always being at my side, stout of heart and revolver in hand, at the times when it really mattered.

More importantly, when do you plan to visit me here? I have no doubt you will find the Sussex climate agreeable this time of year, though spring is almost as delightful and refreshing as the autumn. Your lovely wife is also welcome, although I imagine she certainly would demur at the thought of taking a holiday with me.

Rest assured, Watson, that I am quite at peace these days. I spend my time writing monographs that I had always promised myself to write, and recording the habits of my buzzing queen and her industrious workers – hopefully for the future good of mankind. Yet, I must admit, there are still evenings, when as I smoke my last pipe before retiring, that my mind drifts back to those exciting days we shared lodgings at Baker Street, where I lived off my wits and we were able to assist so many. Now, I am a retired bee-keeper, a scholar of sorts, who has become a worshipper of the salt air. Know one thing, however, that I shall never forget our friendship of the last quarter of a century. Had I one final wish, it would be that just once more, I might cry, 'Hurry Watson! The game's afoot!'

Do come and see me, old fellow. You must know that you are always most welcome ...

and a dear friend who is always in my thoughts.

Very sincerely yours,
Sherlock Holmes

Needless to say, my heart was greatly warmed by Holmes' kind letter, which contained more emotion than I had ever known him to exhibit during our many years together. After reading it, could there be any question what my next move would be?

In spite of my wife's heated protestations, I referred my immediate cases to a colleague for the next fortnight, which allowed me to write about, and live again, the horrors of our extraordinary trip to Chilford on Geoffrey Blake's behalf. Having made some inquiries, I learned that Colonel Collingwood's niece had indeed remarried and started a new life for herself in nearby Acton. Hence, I decided against revealing the facts of her most *outré* mystery, not wanting to cause her any further embarrassment. She had, I felt, suffered enough because of her husband's bizarre sexual habits, and that even with a change of names, I was reasonably certain that there were at least three people still living who would recognise the case immediately, any one of whom might take their stories to Fleet Street for the money the papers would most certainly offer. Therefore, as I tasted my last brandy of the evening, I vowed that the true details of her incredible story must remain undisclosed.

After some thought, I decided to set down, for another day, *The Wilcox Matter* as Holmes had called it, a tale of subterfuge surrounding the death of one of England's most prominent diplomats on the eve of an important trip to the Continent. What amazed me still, as I pored over my notes from so many years before, was Holmes' quick handling of that spurious affair. Seldom have I seen him so accurately perceptive as on that hot summer night, when within hours of being summoned by Inspector Lestrade, he was able to set matters right. Had it not been for his remarkable powers of observation and analysis, I have no doubt the truth would not have been known to this day.

Herewith then, I have recorded the particulars of our visit to Chilford, where Holmes uncovered a mystery that had baffled the Foreign Office and Scotland Yard for years – and solved one of the greatest crimes of the century.

Dr John H. Watson

Watson's sketch of Chilford

ONE

'So Watson, tell me then,' Sherlock Holmes finally asked pointedly, 'what sort of fellow is this Doctor Geoffrey Blake?'

It was an unseasonably cold September afternoon. Outside our comfortable Baker Street lodgings, it was clear a fierce storm was brewing. Already, the streetlamps were being lit, as heavy grey clouds rolled in over the rooftops and darkened the cobblestone streets below.

The weather, I felt, matched Holmes' increasingly restless mood. For the last hour, he had paced to and fro before our crackling fire, impatiently fiddling on his Stradivarius, pausing only from time to time to read, and then read again, a telegram I had received during the morning. The look on his face reflected a growing anticipation.

'I doubt you would find a sounder person,' I replied. 'He certainly comes from a good family. His father, Thurston, you may recall, served for years in the Diplomatic Corps.'

'Ah, there is money in the family, then?'

'I would expect so, yes. But that should not colour your opinion of the man.'

'And why is that?'

'Why, his service record, of course. I first met Blake at Netley, shortly before I was shipped out to Afghanistan. He made it there himself some months later, originally attached to the Royal Northumberlands near Peshawar ... or was it Kabul?'

Holmes put down his violin, and reached again for the telegram that was now the object of his intense scrutiny.

'He saw action, then?'

'Plenty, I would imagine. He also served with the 66th, which took part in the relief of Kandahar under Roberts. The truth is, Holmes, I have not seen Blake for years. But I did hear from a mutual friend, that upon his return from service, he settled in Chilford, near Colchester in Essex.'

Impatiently, he grabbed his black clay from above the fireplace, quickly filled a pipe and sent blue-grey smoke rings swirling towards the ceiling. After which he tossed his tall, gaunt frame onto the sofa.

'You think him no alarmist, then?'

'Absolutely not,' I replied firmly.

'Hmm. Then unless I miss my mark, this is no small matter, for the author of this telegram is most certainly quite perturbed.'

Holmes stared intently at the sheet of paper before him, then thoughtfully began to read it again.

WATSON

MANY YEARS SINCE NETLEY STOP RECALL YOUR FRIENDSHIP WITH SHERLOCK HOLMES STOP MATTERS HAVE COME TO A HEAD STOP MUST SEEK HIS ASSISTANCE AT ONCE STOP SHALL ARRIVE APPROXI-MATELY FOUR PM TODAY STOP DO NOT WISH TO IMPOSE STOP LIVES ARE AT STAKE STOP EVERY HOUR OF THE ESSENCE.

GEOFFREY BLAKE

Holmes gave me an inquisitive glance.

'Come, come, Doctor,' he inquired. 'What are we to make of this?'

'My reaction is the same as when I first read the telegram,' I replied. 'I have always known Blake to be a stalwart fellow. I would guess his problem is quite serious. You read the lines yourself, Holmes. Lives are at stake.'

Holmes sent another cloud of blue smoke swirling.

'Agreed. The manner of his message seems to indicate that he had considered contacting you for a time, yet only now made up his mind to do so.'

'Whatever do you think it was?' I inquired.

Holmes held my gaze with his penetrating, gimlet-like eyes.

'At this point, I will not speculate as to the exact details,' he stated firmly. 'But I will say that murder quite likely is involved. As you so ably pointed out, "lives are at stake". One thing is certain: the man who wrote this telegram is afraid. Read it again for yourself, Watson. Fear exudes from every line.'

The clock on the mantel chimed the quarter hour. Holmes sprang up, strode to the fireplace and re-lit his pipe.

'Not long to wait,' he said, 'it is nearly four. Please ring for Mrs. Hudson, will you? Our visitor has made an arduous journey on this autumn day. He will surely want some tea.'

Holmes' eyes were gleaming, as he cast a glance out of the window at the darkening skies. 'Perhaps,' he added, 'the summer doldrums are at an end.'

Silently I hoped as much. When idle, Sherlock Holmes was not an easy man to live with, and not merely because of the odd hours he often kept. His incredible mind, which thrived on intricate analysis, at the same time deplored the ordinary and commonplace and detested intellectual stagnation. The more difficult the problem, the more cryptic the puzzle, so the more heightened became my companion's incredible powers of deduction. Without the challenge, however, he became easily bored, moody and sullen. Like a spoilt child, he was constantly in need of another new and more interesting toy to stimulate his vivid imagination. When none presented itself, he would go to any length for amusement, including the solution I dreaded most: the needle, kept with a seven percent solution of cocaine in the top drawer of his desk.

Unfortunately, since making his startling return from the dead at the time of the Ronald Adair affair, Holmes had spent a relatively inactive and restless summer. Save for the recent Barrymore kidnapping, and our singular trip to Devonshire on behalf of Bishop Timothy Mayhew in July, few cases had come his way that provided a challenge for his remarkable powers. To combat the inactivity, Holmes had first buried himself in his research, completing informative monographs on powder burns and footprints, after which he began cross-indexing some of his earlier cases that occurred before I made his acquaintance. That being said, I still felt, during the summer of '94, that my friend had been forced to spend far too many hours pacing our rooms and fiddling on his violin than were good for his mental health and general well-being. The latest of my attempts to enlighten his melancholy had been the purchase of two rather expensive front row tickets for a musical that was being performed that very night at the Shaftesbury Theatre, an offer he brusquely refused.

Then had come the telegram. Throughout the day, I had sensed Holmes' excitement quicken.

A few moments before four, we heard the jangling of the front bell, Mrs. Hudson's inquiring voice, and then hurried footsteps upon the stair.

'Come in, Doctor Blake!' Holmes cried, at the sound of a knock upon our door.

Geoffrey Blake's face wore an astonished look as I ushered him inside. His fashionable Albert chain and matching shirt and tie showed him to be a professional man of good standing, and the velvet-lined lapels upon his coat reflected means far more than that of the normal rural physician. His left hand held a gleaming top hat, and blackthorn walking stick. Physically, he had changed little since I saw him last, a solidly built man of medium height, with sandy brown hair and the eyes of the deepest blue. As we greeted, I noted his handshake was firm. And yet, I could tell from his ashen face and agitated manner that something was weighing upon him heavily.

'Good heavens, Mr. Holmes,' he gasped. 'However did you know it was me?'

Holmes' face wore an amused look.

'It was a rather easy deduction,' he replied, 'but hardly an unsound one. Our clients, you see, have been few in recent weeks. And of course, you did say four o'clock.'

Blake nodded with a sigh. 'Ah yes, the telegram. How absurdly simple. My mind, I fear, has not been what it should be the last few days. I am sorry if this forced visit without appointment has inconvenienced you, sir. But given the circumstances, I did not know what else to do. I hope you will understand.'

'No apology is necessary,' Holmes assured him, guiding our visitor to the cane-backed chair in the centre of the room. 'Have a seat close to the fire, won't you? Ah yes, and here is Mrs. Hudson with the tea. Thank you, Mrs. Hudson. Milk or sugar, Doctor?'

As our visitor settled into his chair, Holmes poured Blake a steaming cup, then reposed himself upon our sofa.

'Your countenance,' Holmes observed, 'tells me that you are sorely tried. Obviously, something other than last night's inclement weather has dampened your spirits. Chilford received a good soaking, I presume?'

For a second time, Blake was clearly taken aback.

'How ever did you know?' he demanded. 'I have said nothing about the weather I experienced.'

'Tut, tut. It is all quite elementary,' Holmes replied. 'Your shoes are quite water-soaked at the soles, and splattered with a chalky mud that is not common to the streets of London. The ferrule of your elegant stick is likewise caked, and the wood for nearly an inch above is damp. So you see, it is quite clear that you have traversed puddles and muddy ground this day. When else except when you made your way to catch the train? That you did so in the rain, however, is doubtful, since your coat and hat are dry as parchment. Ergo, heavy rains must have fallen on Chilford during the night, prior to your journey today.'

'By God, sir, you are quite correct!' Blake expostulated. 'Why, I would say you were almost psychic.'

Holmes chuckled. 'No, no, Doctor. I am nothing of the sort, I assure you. My remarks were based merely on simple observation and deduction, which I have found to be an almost infallible process. I can, for example, tell at a glance that you are a Cambridge man with a passion for sailing, who owns a boat, and has spent much time upon the water. You also own a large golden retriever, which you have spoiled incurably. For relaxation, you prefer a Bolivar cigar, at least one of which you enjoyed as you travelled from Colchester.'

Accustomed as I was to my companion's quick methods, I still could not help but be impressed.

'Come, come,' I interjected. 'How on earth do you deduce all that?'

Holmes rolled his eyes.

'It is commonplace, Watson,' he explained. 'Who else but a Cambridge man would wear the Fitzwilliam charm that graces the good Doctor's chain? That he loves the

27

outdoors is clear by his ruddy complexion and the colour of his hair. The sun has brightened all but his sideburns considerably. Note, too, that his hands are calloused which is more common to a field hand than a physician, and that rope burn on his left wrist tells me the wind had recently played him a nasty trick. Combine that with the fact that Clacton and the coast are but a stone's throw from Chilford, and you see my reasoning.' Holmes smiled. 'Besides, a man with velvet lapels can surely afford at least a sleek twelve-footer.'

'But what about the dog and the cigar?' I persisted.

Holmes thrust a hand in my friend's direction.

'How else do you explain the light hairs that adorn his shirt and coat? Clearly, he allows his pet to jump upon him, even when formally attired. His right knee is smudged with cigar ash, most certainly from a Bolivar standard or cabinet-size, an expensive smoke befitting a man of Doctor Blake's position. That the smudges are there at all, I attribute to his long journey in a jostling train compartment, which is a challenge to even the most careful smoker. On this particular morning, I'll wager his thoughts were con-

cerned with matters of far greater importance than the length of his ash.'

Blake, I could see, was clearly impressed.

'Mr. Holmes,' he said sombrely, 'I now
know I made the right decision. You are
most certainly the one person who can help
me in this queer and horrible matter.'

Holmes cast the man a penetrating look.

'Then pray tell us, Doctor,' he inquired.
'Why have you travelled so urgently to
London?'

Blake drew in a long breath.

'Murder,' he said finally. 'No, not just that.
Butchery as well.'

Holmes met my startled glance.

'Go on.'

Blake took a long swallow from his steaming cup before continuing. Outside, heavy
raindrops suddenly began to beat a steady
tattoo upon our bay window. Suddenly
there was a flash of lightning, followed by a
clap of thunder. Our gathering storm had
finally commenced.

Blake set down his cup. His hand, I
noticed, was shaking slightly.

'The facts are these, Mr. Holmes,' he said,
in a forced manner. 'Within a matter of three
days, three residents of Chilford have been
found in their homes brutally murdered.

Trust me, sir, I do not exaggerate! In each case, the victim was stabbed and slashed repeatedly by a fiend who, in my opinion, is not merely content to kill, but must mutilate as well.'

Holmes sent a cloud of blue smoke circling above him.

'Be precise, Doctor,' he instructed. 'These attacks. When did they occur?'

'All at night. At approximately two or three in the morning, as best I can determine.'

'And there was no cry of alarm?'

'No. All three lived alone, you see.'

Homes nodded. 'And the murder weapon?'

'None was found at the scene. But given the size and depth of the wounds, it was most certainly a large knife or dagger. In each case, death was caused by repeated wounds to the throat, chest and stomach. They had all been slashed and stabbed, again and again!' Blake raised his hand to his forehead, and paused a moment before continuing. 'In one case,' he added, 'the stomach cavity actually seemed ... disembowelled.'

'Good Lord!' I exclaimed. 'Surely then, this is the work of a madman, or some type of psychotic.'

Holmes sat poised on the edge of the sofa, his long face grim.

'So it would seem,' he said finally. He strode to Blake's side and placed a steadying hand upon his shoulder. 'I realise the details of this matter may be difficult to recount,' he told our visitor, 'but if I am to be of assistance, it is imperative that you tell me every detail you can recall. Pray, leave nothing out, Doctor. The smallest point, I have found, is often the most essential.'

Blake heaved another sigh. 'You are right of course, sir,' he said. 'I shall give you a full account as best I can.'

'Good man.'

I took the opportunity to fetch Blake what I felt was a needed glass of brandy, for which I received a grateful look of thanks. After a sip or two, he took a deep breath. I was glad to see colour returning to his face. Setting the glass down, he squared his shoulders, as if preparing to undertake some heavy burden, before commencing.

'The first victim was Thomas Harper, the village carpenter,' he continued. 'His apprentice found him in the kitchen behind his shop, on Monday, when he failed to open as usual in the morning. Constable Newton and I were immediately summoned by the lad, and arrived straightaway.

'Mr. Holmes, I am not a squeamish man. As Watson knows, neither the military nor the medical profession will allow it. We both saw much in Afghanistan that is just as well left unsaid. But never in my life, not even during the bloody days near Peshawar, had I seen such deliberate butchery as was before me in Harper's kitchen that day. God as my witness, sir, it shall be in my mind forever.

'The poor man was lying on his back in a large dark pool of his own blood. From throat to waist, he had been cut to ribbons. All round him, the room was a shambles. The table and chairs overturned, dishes smashed, and blood smeared everywhere.' Blake shuddered. 'So stunned was I, that I was sorely tempted to take a bracer from the dead man's bottle.'

A curious expression crossed Holmes' face. 'His bottle?'

'Yes. An open bottle of malt sat on the kitchen counter. Newton concluded that Harper must have been pouring himself a small tot, when the murderer burst in.'

Holmes nodded.

'The front door of his shop was locked then, I take it?'

'Yes, sir. Bolted as well as locked. The lad who summoned us said he had knocked there first, then went around the back when there was no answer. To his surprise, he found the door swung open wide ... and then made his grisly discovery.'

Holmes' eyes narrowed.

'Was there a glass beside the bottle?' he asked.

'No, not that I recall. But why?'

'Nothing, perhaps. Pray, continue.'

'What I am about to tell is the strangest part,' our visitor remarked. 'Neither Newton or I could account for it. Not only had the fiend killed Harper, but he had ransacked the house as well! Pictures were ripped off the walls, lamps broken, even the bed sheets torn apart. I mean, for what purpose, sir? A struggle might account for what we found in the kitchen, but the rest? I can only conclude the killer must have been in a demented rage.'

'The surrounding authorities have been alerted?'

'Oh, yes. And there have been no escapees reported from the district prisons, or the sanitarium in Colchester.'

'And Scotland Yard, I take it, has been notified?'

'Yes. At first, Newton considered this a local matter, but after the second killing, he telegraphed for help immediately. An inspector named Lestrade arrived that very afternoon, and is with us still. Do you know him?'

Holmes smiled thinly.

'Quite well,' he said, taking a long pull at his pipe. 'I have been able to assist him in a number of cases, as Watson will attest.'

I nodded my assent, as Blake gave me an inquiring look.

'Holmes is being somewhat modest in that regard,' I told him, directly. 'If the truth be known, he has aided Lestrade much more than you could imagine.'

Holmes paused thoughtfully.

'Could robbery have been a motive, Doctor?' he asked.

'Perhaps. It was, quite frankly, hard to tell if anything was missing, what with everything being strewn about. But in my opinion, I would discount any thought of theft.'

Holmes regarded the man intently. 'You seem quite certain on that point,' he remarked.

'Harper's tin box was resting on the fireplace, with the key beside it,' Blake informed him. 'Inside, we found a sheaf of notes and

34

coin. I doubt a thief would have left those behind.'

'Hardly,' Holmes concurred. 'And the other two murders? When did they occur?'

Blake took another sip of brandy.

'The second occurred the following night. The victim was Toby Turner, the village handyman of sorts, who lived directly across the street from Harper.' Blake managed a slight smile. 'The cottage wasn't his, of course. But since nobody else wanted it, it became his in fact. The old fellow did farm work and other odd jobs, which earned him his meals and enough to buy a pitcher or two at Weatherby's every night.'

'And on this particular night,' Holmes questioned, 'was he...?'

Blake nodded his head.

'Quite so, according to Mr. Weatherby, who shooed him out of the door just after midnight.'

'Was he killed in the same way?' Holmes asked, matter-of-factly.

'Yes, sir. Stabbed and hacked to pieces, just like Harper. Newton's theory is that the killer was waiting, knowing Toby lived alone, and attacked him once he had stumbled into bed. That was where we found him, still in his clothes.'

'His rooms?'

'The same as Harper's. Things broken and torn to shreds. Not that old Toby had a lot to smash. But the killer did a thorough job, none-the-less.'

'Was there a bottle this time?' Holmes asked.

Blake smiled thinly. 'No, I doubt Toby ever had enough money to purchase a bottle. A pitcher or two of ale was about the depth of his pockets, Mr. Holmes. Again, I feel we can discount robbery as a motive. Save for a few odd carpentry tools, Toby had nothing of worth to steal.'

At that instant, a booming clap of thunder erupted directly above us, causing us all to turn instinctively towards the window. Outside, more lightning flashed, as the rain increased to a heavy gale. As Blake took yet another sip from his glass, Holmes rose and strode to the fireplace, where he re-lit his black clay. Returning to the sofa, he cast our guest a penetrating glance.

'So now we arrive at the point I am most curious to examine,' he commented. 'Who was the person murdered last night? And what was there about that killing that finally compelled you to seek my assistance?'

Blake gave Holmes a questioning look,

which my companion answered with a wave of his hand.

'There is no mystery to my conclusion, Doctor. By your own account, you were shocked by the first murder, and equally so by the second. Yet, in both cases, no missive arrived at our door. Hence, there was something singular to the third killing, which I presume occurred last night, that finally spurred you to action.'

Blake nodded his assent.

'You are correct, of course,' he admitted sadly. 'The third victim was the worst of all. This time, it was a woman.'

'A woman!' I gasped. For a moment, none of us could speak. 'Good Lord, Holmes! It seems we have some sort of "Ripper" here!'

'It was Molly Brighton, a young widow who, like the others, lived alone,' Blake continued. 'Her husband Albert died in a drowning accident, off Clacton just over a year ago. She had since served as housekeeper for Violet McVey, an elderly dowager who befriended her, and allowed her to live in a small cottage she owned beside the river. From my observation, it had seemed a good arrangement, providing Molly with a sound roof above her head, and Violet the care and companionship she required.'

As I hastily took notes of Blake's remarks, I could not help but notice that the rain outside continued to pound down incessantly upon our roof.

'And you found her...?' Holmes inquired.

In one quick motion, Blake drained his glass.

'She was in her bed, poor thing,' Blake responded. 'Without a stitch on, not even a nightdress. She was cut up like the others. God help us all.'

Holmes looked away. I could see, in spite of his attempt to hide his feelings, that he was deeply moved as well.

'I do not mind telling you, sir, I was quite shaken that morning when I saw Newton and Lestrade hurrying up my path,' Blake continued somberly. 'The very look on Newton's face as he approached my door told me why he had come. "There's been another one," he told me. "It's Molly Brighton." For an instant, I was stunned, unable to move. Then somehow, I steadied myself, grabbed my bag, and off we both went.

'I must tell you, gentlemen, that the short walk across the bridge to Molly's cottage was the longest of my life. Newton, I could tell, was also quite affected. So much so that neither of us said a word. One of Lestrade's men was waiting at the door, and as we passed through, I immediately noticed that her things had been strewn about, just like the others. I had expected that. But when I stepped through her bedroom door, and saw her lying amidst the bedclothes in all that blood, those once bright eyes staring blankly up at me...'

Blake grabbed the arm of his chair, and steadied himself before he continued.

'For a moment, I thought I should be ill,' he admitted. 'But I forced myself to kneel down, and examine her ... or what was left of her.' The physician gave me a plaintive look. 'I tell you, Watson, the only thing that got me through was that pledge of loyalty we all took so many years ago, and the responsibilities that it imparts. You know as well as I, no matter what, a doctor must do his duty...'

My friend, I could see, was visibly shaken by his recollection. As quickly as possible, I poured him another brandy.

'You must understand, Mr. Holmes,' he remarked, after taking a sip from his glass, 'that there was another reason why this woman's death affected me so profoundly.'

Thunder shook our windows once again.

'I had suspected as much,' Holmes replied evenly. 'Please continue.'

Blake gave my companion a look of some affront.

'I can assure you, sir,' he retorted, 'it is not any romantic interest that you might suspect. I am, in fact, engaged to one Gwendolyn Tate, who resides in Colchester. We plan to marry at Christmas. She is a splendid creature, and a better marriage there could not be. You have, I am sure, heard of her father, Lawrence Tate, a medical man with some forty years of practice to his credit. In addition to which, he has been a candidate for public office.'

Holmes threw up his hands defensively. 'And I assure you, Doctor,' he insisted, 'that I meant no disrespect. I am merely seeking the facts.'

'The fact is,' Blake said pointedly, 'that Molly and Gwen were close friends. After the banns were announced, Molly took great pains to make Gwen feel welcome in Chilford, introducing her to many of the locals. As you can imagine, I was extremely grateful for that, for residents of small towns can be cliquish to an extreme.' Blake's face wore a look of sadness. 'Molly had broken the ice for Gwen, don't you see?

'Also, there was a great resemblance between them, both being blonde and fair. So much so I felt they could almost pass for sisters. And so, you can imagine my horror, when I saw Molly's curls caked in blood. My first thought, Mr. Holmes, was this might have been my own dear Gwen that morning.'

Holmes gave Blake a curious look. 'You say your fiancée was in Chilford, then?'

'Her father allows her to visit me at times,' Blake explained. 'With a female companion, of course. Gwen and I both love the sea, and sail together when we can off Clacton pier.' His face suddenly hardened. 'God help the fiend who did this,' he added, grimly, 'if ever I can put him in my hands!'

The Doctor gave Holmes a look of agony.

'I knew at that instant I must do something!' he said fiercely. 'Both Newton and Lestrade, it seemed to me, were stymied. Watson, and his friendship with you, came to mind as my only hope. And so, I dashed off and sent the telegram which you received this morning.'

'Your reaction is quite a normal one,' Sherlock Holmes assured him. 'Had I been in your position, I would have done the same. You have, I believe, acted wisely on behalf of your fellow citizens.'

'I must admit, I am glad to hear you say so,' Blake said wearily, 'for I am much the worse for wear at this very moment. Last night I slept badly and even my sleep on the train was horribly disturbed. My dreams were filled with a sleeping woman who was first Molly, then Gwen, suddenly awakened by an intruder at her bedside, throwing up an arm to ward off those awful blows! I awoke in a cold and deathly sweat.'

Blake sank down again into his chair, and took another sip of brandy. He was, I knew, living on his nerves alone.

'If it helps at all,' Holmes said, 'I would offer this consolation: All three victims, remember, lived alone. When your dear Gwen, and her companion, visit you, I assume they reside either in your home, or at a local inn. Hence, I doubt that they are in any foreseeable danger. If anything is clear to me, it is that our murderer chooses his victims carefully. What we must find out is why. That will reveal his motive ... and his identity.'

Holmes thought a little, then regarded our visitor with an intense look. Something, I could tell, had struck a nerve.

'Your dreams cause me to make an inquisitive observation,' he remarked. 'Why do you believe that Molly Brighton threw up just one arm to thwart off her killer's attack? Why just one instead of both?'

'It is my conclusion, based upon the marks found on her body, sir,' he stated, heavily. 'Her left arm and hand were mauled severely, much more so than the right. One finger, in fact, had been severed entirely! Thus, I felt she must have initially thrown up that arm for protection ... although after the first few blows, I doubt she was in any condition to resist.'

While I could not speak for Holmes, the impact of Blake's words hit me like a hammer. For a time, no one said a word. The only sound was the continued pounding of the rain.

Finally, Holmes spoke.

'Which finger was it, if I may ask?'

'Which was...?'

'Yes.'

'The third,' Blake replied.

Holmes' eyes glittered with intrigue.

'And as far as you could determine, nothing of any value had been taken?'

'Not that Newton, Lestrade or I could see,' Blake replied. 'We even asked Gwen and Mrs. McVey to come round and have a look. After the body had been removed, of course.

Their conclusion, Mr. Holmes, was the same. In going through her things, they even found some notes she had hidden away in a dresser drawer. Nothing, it appeared, was missing.'

Holmes put a thoughtful finger to his chin.

'Then robbery, clearly, is not our motive,' he concluded. 'But if not robbery, what then...?

'I mentioned this before, Doctor, but I ask you to be more specific. What about the neighbours? Did any of them report anything out of the ordinary in regards to these three occurrences?'

Blake shook his head. 'No, sir. They did not. And I am certain, Newton questioned them thoroughly on that very point.'

An incredulous look crossed Holmes' lean face.

'You mean to tell me that three horrible murders take place, and not one villager heard a thing? No sounds of a struggle? No screams? No cries for help?'

'I am afraid not,' the physician said. 'And I do believe, if anything had been heard, the person would have spoke up. It would be in their best interests, you must admit.'

'Your point is well taken,' Holmes admitted. 'But still, does it not seem odd to you that no sound of all this violence was heard?'

Blake thought for a second.

'At first, yes,' he concurred. 'But as I mentioned earlier, the scenes of all three murders were somewhat secluded. Harper lived behind his shop, remember. Old Toby's house is the last on the far side of the street. And Molly's cottage is quite isolated ... it sits on the other side of a stream that runs through the town, directly across from the church. It is, as I said, on Mrs. McVey's property, but some distance from her house, as well.'

'I see. Besides the obvious stab wounds, were there any unusual marks or bruises upon the bodies?'

Blake hesitated a moment, a look of uncertainty upon his face. 'No. That is, not that I could tell,' he answered, finally. 'I noticed none when I examined them, but...'

'But you cannot be positive...'

Blake frowned in consternation. 'No,' he admitted, 'but given their mutilated condition, the cause of death seemed clear enough.'

'Yes, I suppose.'

Holmes re-lit his pipe. It was clear to me

he had discovered something and was methodically thinking it through.

'And what is the police theory on this series of brutal attacks?' he asked our guest.

'Originally, they thought them to be the random acts of a deranged person,' Blake responded. 'Someone who has become driven to kill, for whatever mental reason. I, of course, could not fault that logic, for clearly there seems no rhyme nor reason to it all. But the damning point is, who?'

A thought crossed my mind.

'Upon reflection, is there anyone in your town who might have a motive?' I asked. 'Has anyone been acting strangely in recent weeks?'

'Newton and I discussed that very point,' Blake replied. 'To our knowledge, there have been no serious disagreements among the locals recently. Certainly, no feuds or quarrels to provoke anything like this. No, Newton and I both believe it is someone who has recently moved into our midst. Someone quite unknown to us, most likely now in hiding. As to motive, sir, I cannot imagine. I can only pray that we find this killer soon, before, in his demented state, he kills again.'

'When I asked, you said "originally",'

Holmes pressed, 'Someone has changed their opinion, then?'

'Somewhat. Lestrade, you see, is convinced our killer is one of the marsh people ... but tracking them down, I can tell you, will be no easy task.'

'Marsh people?'

'Tramps and gypsies; you know the sort ... they come and they go. Their camps are located in the large marshy areas just north of Chilford, not far off the road that leads to Mersea. There are a number of families and hermits, I am told, in those gloomy woods and marshes, who eke out an existence by hunting and fishing, and cutting reed for thatching. They appear in Chilford, from time to time, to sell their wares, and purchase supplies at John Blair's store.'

Blake withdrew a cigar from his shirt pocket and lit it, before continuing. It was a good sign, I felt, that his mental state was improving.

'I met one of the poor wretches once,' he recalled, 'almost a year ago. The fellow hobbled into my office, dressed in rags, and leaning heavily upon a crutch. He was, quite obviously, in pain. Upon examining him, I found he had broken a leg, which I set, and sent him off without charge. It was, I felt, the least that I could do. He was a friendly sort, but decidedly simple minded. Of course, I daresay I might be so as well, if I spent all my waking hours living in murky waters with bitterns and coots around me.'

Blake's words struck home with me.

'While I do admire your sympathies,' I told him, 'you must admit, it is not un-reasonable to think that someone of that sort, for whatever reason, might go off the deep end, so to speak. Lestrade is correct in that regard, deranged people do quite often strike out irrationally.'

Holmes made no comment upon my remarks, turning his gimlet gaze again to Blake.

'A final question,' he murmured, as he drew heavily upon his pipe. 'Is there anything you can think of that these three victims might have had in common? Some point that might connect these vile atrocities? Take a moment. Think hard, if you will. For it is, as I am sure you understand, quite important.'

There was a long silence, as Blake sat contemplating my friend's question. The only sounds were the crackling of the fire, and the continued noise of the rain outside.

'I must admit, I am at a loss,' the physician said finally. 'If there was a common fact about them, it was only that they all resided in Chilford.'

Holmes smiled faintly.

'Ah, well,' he murmured, 'I had hoped for more. But perhaps something will come to mind later.'

Blake drained his glass and rose to his feet.

'I sense your disappointment, sir,' he remarked, 'but I insist, I have told you all I know. Please, Mr. Holmes, you must help us! There is a vicious killer loose in Chilford. A killer, I feel certain, who will strike again. We must stop him before that happens...' He paused, then added, wearily, 'You must understand, sir. You are my last resort.'

Holmes met Blake's eyes with a steely look that I had seen many times before. I had no doubt what his reply would be, as he rose from the sofa and grasped our visitor's hand.

'Doctor Watson and I shall be glad to offer all possible assistance,' he declared. 'We will catch the nine-fifteen from Liverpool Street station tomorrow morning. If memory serves, we should make Colchester shortly after ten, and I have no doubt we can secure a carriage that will have us in Chilford well before mid-day.'

Blake shook my friend's hand fervently.

'Thank heavens, sir!' he cried. 'You cannot know how relieved I feel, knowing that you are now involved.'

'Given what you have told us, I could contemplate nothing less,' Holmes replied, evenly. 'Most certainly, there is a monster in your midst that must be brought to bay.'

Holmes returned to the fireplace, where he reached for the Persian slipper and began to refill his pipe.

'I do, however, have one suggestion,' he said, as he turned round. 'You must admit, Watson, that our visitor has had an arduous journey this day. I do think a touch of London hospitality is in order. Dinner at The Criterion, perhaps? Oh, and most certainly *The Belle of New York* at The Shaftsbury Theatre! Why, a comedic musical is just the thing to take his mind off this dreadful business.' Holmes gave Blake an amused look. 'I have it on good authority,' he remarked, 'that Watson has two excellent seats in his possession, would you believe for this very night?'

Silently, I chuckled. Holmes' motive, of course, was crystal clear to me. What he desired was time alone, so he could cogitate intently upon the gruesome problem that he had been presented. For my part, I was delighted, as it would give me a chance to re-acquaint myself with my former friend, and insure my considerable investment in the front row seats would not be wasted.

'That is a splendid idea!' I agreed. 'Where will you stay tonight, Doctor?'

'I am told there are always comfortable rooms available at The Northumberland Hotel, at Charing Cross,' Blake replied.

'Excellent!' Holmes interjected. 'Why, even with the heavy evening traffic, you shall have time to freshen up ... and expect Watson to arrive in a hansom at six-thirty. That should provide sufficient time for a relaxed dinner, since the theatre is close by and the curtain does not rise until eight.'

Blake looked disturbed.

'But what about you, sir?' he inquired, as I helped him with his coat and hat. 'Surely, you will at least join us for dinner, then?'

Holmes shook his head.

'There are many compelling aspects to this case I wish to consider,' he explained. 'Regarding dinner, I have no doubt that Mrs. Hudson's larder shall provide most adequately. Watson will tell you that, once I am upon a case, food becomes quite secondary to me. What I require most now is some time with my pipe and violin, so I can think this matter through.'

At the door, Blake extended his hand to Holmes once again.

'Thank you, sir,' he said simply. 'Already, you have eased my worst concerns.'

'Enjoy the evening,' Holmes told him, 'and I shall join you at Liverpool Street station in the morning. Never fear. I shall leave no stone unturned until we set this matter right.'

No sooner had I closed the door, than Holmes was back at the fireplace, a poker in his hand, stirring the burning logs with some agitation.

'Make no mistake, Watson,' he remarked. 'This is a ghastly business. But hardly the work of a madman, I think.'

'However can you make that conclusion?' I asked. While Holmes spoke, I had put away my notebook, and poured myself a glass of brandy. 'I would think that anyone who kills in such a hideous manner must be affected by some sort of aberration.'

'Not so,' Holmes insisted. 'On the contrary, I suspect our killer is both cunning and resourceful, and with a distinct motive in mind.'

'And how do you deduce that?'

'A madman wielding a knife would hardly

take the time to silence his victims before-hand. Yet that must be the case, or some cry of surprise, pain or terror would have been heard. In each case, I'll wager, the victim was either knocked unconscious or strangled before the mutilation. Why, Blake all but admitted it! Given the bloody scene he encountered, a bump on the head or bruises upon the throat were the last thing he would have looked for. That is the only possible explanation, Watson. The real cause of death was concealed by mutilation.'

'But why?'

'Time, Watson. Time is what the killer sought. To mutilate a body and ravage rooms to the extent our visitor described is no quick task. Had any of the victims cried out, help was only as far as a neighbours' abode. The killer could not afford that anyone should hear, hence he made certain that no cry was uttered, no alarm sounded, that might keep him from his grisly business. Yet, if he were a fiend or lunatic, why should he care?'

'Yes,' I said, 'I think I am beginning to see what you mean.'

'There is cold, cruel logic behind these crimes,' Holmes continued, relighting his pipe. 'Of that, I am certain.' He frowned.

'The trouble is, I do not at present have enough pieces of the puzzle in hand. My fear is, before I do, that our killer will strike again.'

'Even now,' I queried, 'that Scotland Yard is on the scene?'

'Lestrade and a dozen constables would not deter this man,' Holmes remarked, grimly. 'Two things seem clear to me. He has a plan, and he is bold. Which makes him all the more dangerous.'

I took a sip from my glass. What I sought was some additional light upon what Holmes was thinking.

'But surely,' I commented, 'there must be more upon which you base your speculation than the manner in which these people died.'

Holmes sent another cloud of blue smoke upward.

'Speculation, you say?' he remarked. 'What about the bottle in Harper's kitchen? What about the open moneybox? Why, in all three instances, were the victims' possessions gone through, yet nothing of value stolen?'

'Those points are well taken,' I admitted.

'Think about it, Watson! If the murderer had burst in on Harper as Blake suggested, he is more likely to have dropped the bottle, or thrown it at his attacker. But to calmly set it down upon the counter? That, I find, beyond the realm of probability. That the entire kitchen was torn asunder, and yet that bottle survived intact? That you cannot classify as even a miracle ... it is a sheer impossibility.'

'Your conclusion, then?'

'The only thing that could have happened,' Holmes stated, 'is that after killing Harper, the murderer procured the bottle from a shelf or cupboard, then helped himself to a drink. It was, I think, to steel himself for the grisly work that lay ahead.'

'And the moneybox beside the fireplace?' I inquired.

'People hardly keep their savings on display,' Holmes declared. 'My guess is that the killer sought something besides money from that box. Upon retrieving it, he either took it with him, or destroyed it in the fire.' Holmes gave me a knowing look. 'The point is, Watson, he knew where to find the bottle, and what was in that box...'

'If that is the case,' I exclaimed, 'it can mean only one thing. The killer knew his victim well!'

'Exactly.'

I frowned. 'And yet, something bothers me

here,' I questioned. 'What about Turner and Molly Brighton? According to Blake, Turner had nothing of value, and the woman's money was found intact. Following your logic, what might they have possessed that the killer sought? It is, I admit, too deep for me to fathom.'

Holmes thought briefly.

'That is the puzzling part,' he said, finally. 'There seems to be a pattern here, and yet, upon close examination, there is not. Certainly, the method of killing was the same. The victims were silenced and then mutilated. After which, their abodes were ransacked, as if by a madman upon a rampage. But regarding motive or gain, I can fathom no connection.' Holmes took another puff upon his pipe. 'But mark my words, Watson, there is one, and when we find it, we shall have our murderer.'

Holmes strode to the coat rack next to our door where, to my surprise, he plucked his Penang lawyer from the stand.

'Are we off somewhere then?' I inquired, dubiously. 'It is still pouring, you know.'

'Not at all,' my friend assured me, as he returned to my side. 'But there is one other singular point of Blake's testimony that bothers me. Lie down upon the sofa, would you, so I may illustrate?'

So surprised was I at my friend's suggestion, that I nearly spilt my glass.

'Lie down upon the sofa?' I expostulated. 'But whatever for?'

'You are Molly Brighton,' Holmes explained, as I put down my glass and did as he requested, 'and asleep in your bed. I am the murderer, who suddenly appears above you...'

In a flash, Holmes raised the stick above his head and slashed downward at my chest. Instinctively, I threw up my arms to shield myself from the blow. But just as quickly, Holmes grabbed my left hand and held it fast. Dropping the stick, he tapped on my hand gently, first top and bottom, and then side to side.

'You do see my point?' he inquired, releasing my hand. 'No matter from what angle the blows were struck, there is no way my weapon could have severed your third finger, without taking off at least the little finger as well.'

I could not help but shudder at the import of his conclusion.

'Then her finger must have been purposely cut off,' I deduced. 'My God, for whatever reason?'

'It is the ring finger, Watson,' Holmes explained, grimly. 'Thus, I would ask you to cogitate along those lines. We are in deep waters here, make no mistake. Quite deeper than your friend Blake would ever think.'

Holmes' sobering conclusion left me numb. Without a word, I drained my glass and left the room to dress for the evening.

TWO

The following morning, I awoke a little after six. My evening at the theatre with Blake, as well as a few glasses of The Criterion's best, had revived my spirits, and I felt remarkably refreshed. During the night, the storm had passed. Now, bright sunlight streamed through my bedroom window, flooding the room with a pleasant warmth that hastened me to my ablutions, eager to meet the fresh autumn day.

Holmes, I recalled as I quickly shaved and dressed, had hardly noticed me when I arrived back at our abode the night before. Sitting by the fire in his chair, he had seemed lost in thought, scratching morosely on his violin. My greetings, as I entered, were met by silence. Knowing his mood, I realised any attempt at conversation would be impossible, and so grabbed a volume of my favourite sea stories from the shelf and ambled off to bed.

Now I found, as I approached the table where he sat, that his mercurial temperament had turned full circle to match the brightness of the morning. His plate of eggs, toast and bacon, I also noticed, had scarcely been touched.

'Ah, there you are Watson!' he proclaimed heartily. 'Released from arms of Morpheus, at last! Sit down, sit down. Mrs. Hudson has, as usual, provided most generously to our needs, including a jar of strawberry jam that I am certain you will find mouth-watering.'

'You seem decidedly cheerful this morn-ing,' I replied, somewhat testily. 'When I returned last night, you would not speak. You just sat there at the fire, scratching away on your infernal violin. Have you discovered something, then, that has improved your mood?'

Holmes chuckled, and put down the copy of *The Times* he had been reading.

'My profound apologies, dear Watson,' he implored. 'I was, I must admit, much pre-occupied with our present conundrum. But surely, after all these years, you have come to recognise my moods. If, at times, I seem unreceptive to social conversation, it is simply because I am so deeply involved in the problem at hand.' Holmes surveyed his plate, but decided upon a sip of coffee instead. 'How was the play, then?'

'I found it rather disappointing,' I admitted, as I helped myself to a portion of eggs and bacon. 'It was a silly tale about an American woman and her romance with a sailor. Not on a par with Gilbert and Sullivan, to be sure.' I reached for a slice of toast, then adorned it with butter and jam. 'Blake, however, seemed to enjoy it immensely. I guess that was the important thing.'

Holmes smiled with amusement.

'As much as you enjoyed the performance of Miss Cynthia Dennis?' he inquired.

I felt a flush of colour rush to my cheeks.

'And what do you mean by that?' I sputtered. 'Why, she has a fine voice, most certainly, But apart from that...'

Holmes laughed heartily.

'My dear Watson!' he cried, tossing his napkin aside. 'There is no need for such embarrassment. Your taste when it comes to the weaker sex has always been impeccable. Based on your actions, I must conclude that Miss Dennis' performance was quite impressive, even though she was only the second lead.'

'And how did you deduce that?' I demanded.

'Why, by the programme you left upon the desk,' Holmes explained. 'Not only did you underline her name twice, but you circled it for good measure.'

Rising, he went to the fireplace, grabbed his black clay and the Persian slipper, and lit his first pipe of the day.

'The Dover sole?' he inquired. 'It was far better than the play, I take it?'

'And how do you know I ordered Dover sole?' I asked, defensively

'Because, dear Watson, you are an incurable creature of habit,' my friend replied. 'Should you, when dining at The Criterion, order anything but their delicious Dover sole, braced with rice and a decanter of white wine, I will be amazed, indeed! How many times have we supped there in the last two years, and always it is the same. Dover sole, rice, and an exquisite Chablis.'

'Bother my Dover sole,' I told him, as he returned to the table, sending clouds of blue smoke through the shafts of sunlight that crossed our room. 'What about these horrible murders, Holmes? Was your night of pipe and violin productive? Have you, indeed, made some progress?'

Holmes seemed chagrined.

'Painfully little, I am afraid,' he said.

'Certainly there is a method to this business, but I am becoming more convinced it is the method that is deceiving. I sense that our killer has created the "Chilford Ripper" in order to cover up a much deeper motive. But what it is, I've no idea. Yet my very being tells me that each of these three killings was committed for a different reason.'

'And why is that?'

'Because after the method, Watson, all similarities end. The answer, I am convinced, lies in the murder of Thomas Harper. He was the first, remember? That killing was an action. The second, I suspect, was a reaction.'

'Whatever do you mean?'

'Toby Turner, I am convinced, was murdered solely because of what he saw, or what the killer thought he saw, as he wandered home from the inn. It forced the "Ripper" to strike quickly ... the very next night, in fact, to silence a possible witness. Blake told us, remember, that Turner lived directly across the street from Harper, and that he normally left the inn at a late hour. That would put him near Harper's house at the time of the murder. Perhaps he passed out in the street, and was awakened by the row. Who knows? But it seems to be the only explanation that fits.'

'But what about Molly Brighton?' I queried. 'She lived nowhere near the other two.'

'A sad case,' Holmes said. 'I suspect she was the murderer's mistress.'

'What!' I exclaimed. 'But how can you deduce...'

Holmes silenced me with a wave of his hand.

'It was the third finger, Watson, remember? What more likely than a ring?'

'A ring?'

'A ring the killer really wanted to retrieve. So much so, that in desperation he was forced to cut off her finger to get it. Why he decided to kill her, I have no idea. But once he did, he decided to let the "Chilford Ripper" again take the blame. It was, I suspect, only after he had completed his grisly task that he remembered to remove the ring. Unfortunately, by then, *rigor mortis* had begun to set in.'

'Come, come, Holmes,' I interjected. 'Molly Brighton was a widow, after all. They often continue to wear their wedding ring, after a husband's death. Is it not more likely that the killer stole the ring for its value?'

Holmes gave me a disparaging look.

'And left behind a box containing notes

and coins that he would have no trouble spending?' he replied. 'No, Watson, that explanation just will not do. The ring Molly Brighton was wearing had some special significance, rather than monetary value.'

'So she, like Harper, knew the killer then?'

'Quite intimately, I would suspect. Think, Watson! Two people have been brutally murdered within two nights. A woman alone is not likely to simply open her door to anyone. My guess is that she was quite welcome for his company upon that night.' Holmes sighed. 'Poor thing. Instead of protection, he turned upon her. But why?'

For a moment, as I finished my eggs and bacon, I ruminated on all that Holmes had told me.

'I must confess,' I said, finally, 'that I feel you may be straying a little far afield in this.'

Holmes shook his head.

'No, Watson. As I have told you many times, the science of deduction is simple and exact. Eliminate all other factors, and what remains, no matter how implausible at first glance, must be the truth. Nothing, I've found, is more deceptive than an obvious fact, simply because people tend to overlook it.'

'I do suppose you are right,' I conceded. 'I

wonder what Blake will think of your reasoning.'

'For the moment, Watson, I would prefer that your revealed nothing of what we have said to Doctor Blake, or anyone else, for that matter.'

Holmes' request caught me by surprise. 'But surely, you don't suspect...'

'What I suspect,' Holmes interrupted, glancing at his watch, 'is that unless you hurry, we will miss our train. It is nearly eight, now, and I have already made arrangements. A hansom will be at our door at eight-thirty. My bag is packed, but I doubt you can say the same.'

'Holmes,' I fumed, tossing down my napkin, 'there are times you treat me like a schoolboy. How many times have we departed thus? Never fear, I shall have my bag in hand, when our transport arrives.'

'Be sure to include your service revolver, Watson,' my friend replied. 'I have no doubt we shall have need of it. One thing is sure ... we are dealing with a ruthless killer, whose plan, I feel, is not yet complete. We must be ready, when he decides to strike again.'

THREE

Liverpool Street station was, as to be expected, very busy at that hour of the day. Already, throngs of people were gathered in the street level concourse above the terminus, situated on the corner of Liverpool Street and Bishopsgate, and more were alighting from hacks and carriages in the bright morning sun. Our hansom deposited us beneath the tower and giant clock of The Great Eastern Hotel, which overlooked the dual entrances to Liverpool Street, whose 18 platforms made it the largest station in London.

On securing a porter for our bags, we entered the cavernous station and followed him along the small corridor that connected what, in fact, were two stations under one roof of iron and glass, the west and east side being separated by the rails of platforms nine and ten, which split it up the middle and were only connected by a walkway overhead. After descending the stairs to the platform area, we continued on past the general offices of the Great Eastern Railway to platform nine, where the train to Colchester and Ipswich awaited departure.

As always, I was depressed by what I considered the uninspired architecture and gloomy atmosphere of the place, upon which a vast fortune had been spent, over the years, in renovations. It was a colossal mistake, I felt, since the terminal was only a stone's throw from Old Jago, one of London's foulest slums, which was inhabited almost entirely by criminals of every sort; pickpockets, burglars and prostitutes.

As we walked along, I noted that Liverpool Street, because the starting point for its departing trains was at the bottom of an incline, retained more than its fair share of smoke and grime from the steam of the waiting engines, whose impatient beat of Westinghouse brake pumps so often turned what little sunlight filtered down through the glass roof into a misty fog, not unlike that which so often blanketed the streets of London.

Knowing Holmes' penchant for reading on the train, I stopped at a newsagents, where I purchased copies of *The Times*, *Pall Mall Gazette* and the previous night's *Evening Standard* – while he marched on ahead.

'It looks as if half of London rose early this morning, Holmes,' I remarked, when I joined him on the platform moments later. 'I doubt there are enough worms for all the early birds this day.'

'It is a Friday, remember,' Holmes replied. 'And the weather has turned most fair. I would judge we are witnessing the last exodus to the coast, Watson, before the damp and fogs of winter set in. As well as the normal everyday travellers, many of these people are taking belated holidays to Clacton or Mersea, unless I miss my guess. Anxious for one last sunny weekend by the sea.'

He glanced down at the newspapers in my hand, as the crowds of people bustled past.

'Anything of interest?' he inquired.

'I did not have a chance to read much,' I answered. 'But according to the headline, the Home Secretary is off to the Continent again. The French, it seems, have the wind up over something.'

'Most likely it is the Crown Prince's unannounced visit to Bosnia,' Holmes remarked. 'Europe is, after all, an armed camp and any new alliance concerning Germany would certainly tip the scales against the French.'

It was at that moment that Blake appeared beside us, with a porter beside him.

'Thank goodness, I found you,' he exclaimed. 'I was beginning to think you must have been delayed. Porter, take their bags, will you? I took the liberty of reserving a compartment, Mr. Holmes.'

'Perfect,' my friend replied. 'If you will show the way...?'

Moments later, we were ensconced in our compartment. Holmes, as was his habit, lit a pipe, then immediately began to peruse the agony column of *The Times*.

'If this weather holds, Watson,' Blake remarked, 'we shall have a fine shot at some partridge this afternoon. It is the least I can do in return for your kindness of last night. But I warn you, Chilford birds are remarkably quick and tricky.'

'No more so, I imagine, than Scottish grouse,' I replied, heartened at the positive change in Blake's demeanor. 'A sovereign says I shall fill my bag.'

'For sport, I will take that wager,' Blake replied. 'We can settle up over a glass of brandy when we return from the fields.'

At a little after nine-fifteen, our compartment gave a shudder, as the train proceeded to pull slowly out of the station and through the drab railway yards that pointed east. The scene was certainly a depressing one – old grey warehouses of faded brick, with windows so stained and grimy that I doubted even this day's bright sun could penetrate the panes. How could anyone, I wondered, work within those bleak confines and not feel discouraged with their lot in life?

Within minutes, thankfully, we had left the drab greys of central London behind, and were steaming east through the suburbs of Stratford and Ilford. Holmes, as I expected, said not a word, so buried was he in the morning papers. Blake, who had procured a pack of playing cards, proceeded to teach me a new and fairly simple game called gin, which rewarded one's ability to build up runs and match three or four of a kind. After a few hands, which I won, I felt comfortable enough to accept my friend's offer of a penny a point and a shilling to the winner.

'How did you happen to settle in Chilford?' I asked him, as he dealt another hand. 'Your family is from Dover, after all. It was hardly in your neck of the woods, you must admit.'

Blake smiled.

'Certainly not by plan,' he explained. 'Upon returning from India, I had set up practice in Dover, but to be honest, the going was rather slow. Two years ago, on advice from a colleague, I decided to holiday in Mersea. Riding down from Colchester, I passed through a small town at the edge of a thick wood, where the road crossed a fast-moving stream. When I inquired, the driver told me it was Chilford. "It is a pretty enough place," he admitted, "but there's not much to it. Quiet as the end of the Earth."

'Still, my curiosity was aroused. So I climbed down and walked about for a while, taking in the stares of the locals, as you might imagine, and sampled an ale at Weatherby's. Well, not to make too fine a point of it, but the place took hold of me. Later that week, I returned, and ended up spending more time there than at the coast, before my return to Dover...'

'Gin!' I announced, 'A run of spades, plus sixes and sevens. So, you moved right in, then?'

'It would be a nice story,' Blake replied, 'but that was not the case. You see, there was already a physician in Chilford. Ferguson, by name. And it was clear to me that the town was much too small to support two practices. So I continued on, as best I could, in Dover.'

'I see. But then, what occurred to change your situation?'

'Last spring, I received a telegram from Stephen Langley, whose acquaintance I had made during my stay. Ferguson, he informed me, had died quite suddenly ... thrown from his horse while riding ... and he was inquiring if I might have an interest in setting up a practice there.'

'Langley?' I pondered, as I perused my cards. 'I have heard that name before.'

'Most certainly, if you are a horseman,' Blake remarked, 'he is the owner of Briarwood Stables, located just to the north of the town...'

'But, of course! It is the home of *Noble Duke*, and before that, *Forrester*, both winners of The Wessex Cup, as I recall.'

Blake, to my consternation, picked up my third straight discard.

'You are correct,' he stated. 'Briarwood has been in Stephen's family for decades. His father, I am sorry to say, died while he was in service. Stephen took control upon his return. At any rate, I gave Langley's offer a few days thought, then telegraphed back, "Why not?" Ferguson's house, I found, was available at a reasonable price. So I purchased it from the widow, and took up country life.'

Blake drew another card, then threw down

his hand.

'Gin.'

'Fives and sixes,' I remarked, with a frown. 'No wonder I could not fill my run. Wait a minute, it seems we are slowing down.'

Holmes put down his paper and glanced out of the window.

'We are arriving at Chelmsford,' he informed us. Holmes pulled his watch from his waistcoat pocket. 'On time, too,' he added. 'At this rate, we should make Colchester in 20 minutes, at the most.'

By the time our train pulled out of the station, Blake had quickly put down his cards twice more – relieving me of a shilling and several pennies before he dealt another hand. Holmes, after assuring us as to why any immediate treaty between Germany and Bosnia was unlikely to occur, lit a fresh pipe, then plucked up his copy of *Pall Mall Gazette* and disappeared behind its pages.

Blake's mastery of the game continued, as he won the first two hands.

'I am impressed, I must admit,' I told him. 'There is, clearly, more to this game than meets the eye.'

My friend chuckled.

'The key is knowing when to play defensively,' he said. 'I have found you cannot always count on the luck of the draw.' Blake paused to light a Bolivar, then added, 'I have no doubt you will master it in time. But for now, I do have an advantage, since I have been playing this game for some time.'

'And who taught you?' I asked, as I sorted through my cards.

'Langley,' Blake replied. 'He and his friends brought it back from India. Out there, it was always hard to find a fourth for whist, you see. So some bright subaltern devised a two-handed game. I'm told it caught on like wildfire in the ranks. It was originally played for drinks, not money. Hence the name.'

'Ah! And where did Langley serve then?'

'He and his friends were with a supply unit in Bombay. Rather quiet, he told me. Nothing like we experienced in the north, although there were some native disturbances, from time to time.'

'You keep referring to his friends,' I observed. 'I take it, then, a number of ex-soldiers now reside in Chilford?'

Blake sent a cloud of smoke towards the ceiling, as he contemplated his hand. 'Quite so. There were five of us, including myself, before Harper's demise. The other four served with Langley in Bombay. We meet every other Saturday, for a game of cards.'

Blake's eyes clouded. 'But after Harper's death, I think no one will feel much like it, as I'm sure you can understand.'

'But, of course.'

Blake drew and discarded.

'Yes,' he said, 'I imagine it will be some time before The Cooper Club meets again.'

'The Cooper Club?'

'That is what we call ourselves,' Blake explained. 'It is in honour of a fallen comrade, whom the four brought back to Chilford for a proper burial when they were discharged.'

As an ex-serviceman, I found Blake's explanation touching.

'That is quite commendable,' I remarked, 'but I would have thought his family would have settled his final affairs.'

'As I was told, he had none,' Blake explained. 'No brothers or sisters, and his parents both deceased. His name was Harry Cooper, who like Harper was from Bristol. He was ambushed during a food riot, shortly before they were due to be discharged. Harper was at Cooper's side at the time he was attacked, and promised him as he was dying that he would rest in English soil.'

'I see.'

'So, they brought him back and buried him in Chilford. Stephen, I'm told, arranged the funeral, and paid for all expenses, including a huge obelisk that marks the grave. It is an impressive stone. I do not exaggerate when I tell you that it stands at least fifteen feet in height! You cannot help but notice it, even from a distance.'

Blake sighed at my discard and drew again.

'I shall never forget the night they decided upon the name,' he remarked. 'Even looking back today, it still seems strange.'

'Whatever do you mean?'

'It was the first night I had joined them for cards, late in the evening, with many hands played, and more than a few drinks as well. Langley was the one who brought it up. "Gentlemen," he said, "we are rather an unlikely group, you must admit, but given our service to the Queen, I think we deserve a name. What shall we call this club, then?"'

Blake smiled as he drew his next card, before continuing.

'For a moment, nobody said a word. Then Harper gave Langley a look and said, "Why! The Cooper Club, of course. The Cooper Club in honour of poor old Harry!"'

'I am sure all present were touched by that sentiment,' I intoned.

Blake set down his cards, an amused look

upon his face.

'No, Watson, that is my point. The reaction of the others was anything but sombre. At first, Langley seemed taken aback, and then he began to laugh!'

'Laugh?' I ejaculated. 'I cannot believe it...'

'Neither could I. But then the others started laughing as well. Not knowing what to say, I just smiled and went along with them. Then Langley raised his glass and proposed a toast.

'"Harper, you rogue," he said, "you have hit the nail on the head! The Cooper Club it shall be." After which, we toasted the poor fellow's memory and the cards were dealt again.'

'How extraordinary,' I told him. 'Did you ask for an explanation?'

'No,' Blake replied, 'but I sensed there was a deeper meaning there, something they as comrades held between them. Since no one volunteered, I felt it was not my place to ask.'

As Blake was speaking, Holmes put down his paper, a thoughtful expression upon his lean face.

'You will pardon my interruption,' he said to Blake, 'but I find it peculiar. Why would

Langley's friends all decide to return with him to Chilford? I would have thought they would have scattered to the sundry towns of their birth, once their ship made port.'

'According to Langley,' Blake explained, 'their mass exodus was anything but planned. Originally, he extended an invitation to stay on a while at Langley Hall. After a time, I imagine, they came to like the place and put down roots like myself.'

'And what are their professions? Work, I would think, would be hard to come by in such a remote community.'

'Langley, I was told, supported Archer in a tobacco shop, and secured Hastings a position with Miles Thorne, the town smithy. Harper had been a carpenter prior to entering service, so Langley had his tools brought up by train from Bristol and he set up shop.'

'And they have all done well?' Holmes asked.

'Remarkably so,' the Doctor replied. 'Now that I think of it, I have never seen any of them short of funds. Archer, in fact, is known for his willingness to buy a round of drinks at the inn, once the evening gets late.'

'My, my,' Holmes mused. 'By your account, they do seem a close-knit group, indeed.'

Blake gave my friend an inquisitive look, as if trying to determine the motive of his remark.

'Why, yes they are, now that you mention it,' he replied. 'And yet, I must tell you, sir, I do not find that strange at all. As Doctor Watson will attest, the bond between those who have served together often goes beyond mere friendship.'

'Blake is right there, Holmes,' I stated. 'Why, take Murray for example. Had he not thrown me across his packhorse when I was wounded at Maiwand, I should not be here today. My resources are not considerable, but should he seek assistance, I doubt I could refuse.'

Holmes nodded in agreement. 'And rightly so, dear Watson,' he said. 'Rightly so. One other thing, Doctor,' he said to Blake. 'When was it exactly that these four soldiers returned to Chilford?'

'On that I cannot be certain,' the Doctor stated. 'But it had to be before I first took a holiday there two years ago. I clearly remember Archer's tobacco shop on that visit, and sharing a pint with Langley at the inn.' Blake paused. 'Wait a minute! Now that I think of it, I recall Harper once saying it was an unusually cold September when they returned.

That the leaves were turning and there was an unseasonable bite in the air.'

'Which means,' Holmes mused, as if talking to himself, 'that they could have been discharged as early as summer 1892...'

'Yes. But why?'

Holmes shrugged. 'Oh, a coincidence, most likely,' he replied, cryptically, as he disappeared again behind his paper. 'Your remarks brought quite another matter to mind.'

Upon arriving in Colchester, we had little trouble securing a sturdy four-wheeler for the journey east to Chilford. It was as enjoyable a ride as I have ever taken. The day was sunny and bright, warm enough, in fact, that we chose to discard our heavy outer coats before climbing aboard. Holmes lit another pipe as we clattered off, while Blake enjoyed a fresh cigar.

For over an hour, we travelled through rich, undulating farm country, enjoying the fresh air and pastoral scenery – lush green pastures and wooded hillsides that seemed to stretch on as far as the eye could see. In one such field, a herd of black-faced Suffolks watched us curiously as we passed, and more than one farmer's dog – alerted, no doubt, by the approaching clip-clop of our horses' hooves – charged out to the road to greet us, barking furiously.

Further on, at the edge of one freshly ploughed field, a deserted white windmill stood lonely guard, its blades creaking slowly in the breeze. Not long after, I suddenly noticed the smell of the North Sea in the air, and observed a flock of seagulls circling over what appeared to be flat, murky marshlands ahead.

'The coast cannot be far off,' I observed, 'the wind is from the east, and salty.'

'You are correct,' Blake told me. 'Chilford is just over this next hill, and Mersea but a few miles distant.'

Holmes, who had said little during our relaxing journey, suddenly broke his silence.

'I can well understand your affection for this country, Doctor,' he commented, wistfully. 'The atmosphere is quite peaceful here. It has an attractive loneliness that many would not appreciate. I have already decided, in my declining years, to retire to an area as remote as this. A place in Sussex comes to mind where I shall devote what time is left to me to the study of bees.'

Blake's features became grim. 'Chilford was quite peaceful once,' he remarked, dourly. 'I can only hope, someday, it will be so once again. I do not wish to intrude, but I must ask you, now that you have given this matter some thought; what conclusions have you formed about these horrors?'

'A few,' Holmes replied. 'I am convinced that while the method of these murders is the same, they are in no way related. And that they are hardly the crimes of a maniac, or a deviant. Cruel logic is involved in this ... and motive is the key.'

'Ah, you have formed a theory, then?' Blake persisted, hopefully.

'Vague outlines, nothing more,' Holmes informed him, 'and until I possess more facts, they are not worth the time to mention. I will say that we are a long way off and time, unfortunately, is not on our side.'

In spite of the bright sunshine, I shuddered. My thoughts, upon Holmes' words, were equally grim. What had happened, I wondered, in the twenty-four hours since Blake set off for London? What progress had Lestrade and Newton made? Had they apprehended the killer, or was he still at large?

'One thing,' Holmes asked, interrupting my thoughts. 'I assume that Chilford possesses a telegraph office?'

'Yes, Mr. Holmes. There is a connection at

the shop of Edward Lattimer, the town undertaker.'

'Excellent. Then I shall want you to introduce me to Mr. Lattimer, as soon as we arrive. I had wanted to speak with him, in any case, but while I am doing so, I shall also send off a telegram.'

Upon hearing this, I was unable to withhold my curiosity.

'But to whom?' I asked.

'My brother, Mycroft. In order to prove the veracity of my conjectures, I shall need to make use of his considerable government connections.'

Both Blake and I were clearly taken aback.

'Government connections?' I cried. 'Whatever has the government to do with this? Holmes, you have lost me now, I must admit...'

Holmes smiled. 'I myself may be the one who is lost,' he ruminated. 'At present, I am still sorting through the facts and trying to verify which are true and which are not.'

Given Blake's earlier remarks, I could not help but comment on Lattimer's seemingly diverse occupations.

'How does a man become both undertaker and telegram operative?' I inquired. 'That is a strange combination, you must admit.'

Blake chuckled. 'Lattimer wears many hats,' he informed us. 'He is an industrious soul, to be sure. He also keeps the town records, and is the keeper of the park and cemetery.'

As we approached the crest of a low hill, Holmes pursued another line.

'From what you have related,' he told Blake, 'I take it that Thomas Harper was not married. Did he have any, shall we say, female companions?'

'More than a few,' Blake said, with some disdain. 'His latest was a plain-looking red-head from Coggeshall. What he saw in her, I can only guess.' He inhaled deeply on his cigar. 'It seems clear she cared little for him, however. She did not even attend his funeral.'

'And what about the others? Archer, Hastings and your friend Langley?'

'Archer keeps company with a woman named Meg Pryor, who waits at tables in the inn. Hastings likes his ale, but is no ladies' man. A man of Langley's wealth would be quite a catch, but I know of no serious relationships.' Blake smiled. 'I do know, however,' he added, 'that he makes occasional trips to London. But what he does there is not my business to ask.'

'One other point,' Holmes inquired. 'Who did you tell that you were travelling up to consult with me on Thursday?'

'Why, only Newton and Weatherby,' Blake answered, defensively, 'and Gwendolyn, of course.'

Holmes frowned.

'Then by now,' he concluded, 'the killer must certainly suspect we are *en route*.'

'Here, now!' Blake burst forth. 'What is it you are implying?'

Holmes calmed the man with a wave of his hand.

'Only that in a town as small as Chilford, nothing remains a secret for long,' he said evenly. 'It is human nature, after all. You must realise, Doctor, that if my present suspicions are correct, this matter is far from being concluded. News of your journey, I fear, might cause the killer to accelerate his timetable. We can only hope that is not the case.'

Our horses strained one final time as our carriage crested the rise. Suddenly, ahead, we could see a cluster of shopfronts and houses that I took to be Chilford – nestled between thick dark woods on one side, and flat, grassy pasture lands on the other. As Blake had described, a fast-moving stream cut through the centre of the town, its blue waters sparkling in the sun. With the low hill behind us, the horses instinctively quickened their pace, so much so that our driver had to rein them in a little as we approached. A square stone bridge, I observed, crossed the stream that divided the town. On the left stood an ancient stone church with a piercing spire, with a small cemetery behind. On the right side of the stream, only two structures could be seen – a large gabled house set back from the road, and a small thatched cottage, somewhat closer to the bridge.

'I take it that is the McVey property on the right,' I said to Blake, 'and that the cottage was where Molly Brighton resided.'

'You are correct,' he replied, sadly. 'The cottage, I'm told, was not much when Molly took it over some years ago. But she got it ship shape in no time at all. All thatched and painted, with the white fence and flower beds. She was quite proud of it, Gwen told me once, as well she should have been.'

'Roses,' Holmes commented. 'A pleasant touch, to be sure. But such improvements must have taxed her dearly on a servant's pay. Ah, well! Perhaps Mrs. McVey lent a hand.' For a moment, Holmes gazed about at the pastoral scene around us. 'Chilford,' he observed to Blake, 'is most certainly as you described it. I doubt I have ever seen a more picturesque country town.'

'And yet,' Blake remarked, 'you must admit, a picture with a darker side at present. Who would think that it concealed such ghastly acts of murder?'

'As is usually the case with the troubles of our world,' my friend replied, 'the cause lies not with nature, but with man.'

Blake pointed towards a large, grey house that set upon some high ground at the edge of the woods, overlooking the church and cemetery. 'That is Langley Hall,' he told us. 'The home of the family for three generations. The stables and pastures are located on the flats behind. The view from the house is quite impressive, albeit somewhat sobering.' Blake raised an arm and pointed. 'And there's the obelisk.'

As we passed, I was amazed at the size of the tall dark monument that Blake had mentioned on the train. It was a towering thing, standing next to a mausoleum that dominated the otherwise flat expanse of grass dotted with headstones.

'Your description most surely did it justice,' I remarked, 'but it seems a bit ostentatious, I must say.'

'I will be honest, it did cause some disagreement,' Blake admitted. 'The other comrades were of your opinion, Doctor Watson. But Langley was dead set about the type of stone he wanted and, since he was incurring the cost, they all finally went along.'

'And what about Harper?' I asked. 'What sort of monument marks his grave?'

'A plain granite headstone has been ordered,' Blake replied, defensively. 'I know what you are thinking. I felt the same. But, as I'm sure you understand, if the other three were in agreement, it was not my place to question.' Blake paused, then added, 'But he does lie next to Cooper. They all felt that was appropriate.'

Before I could reply, Holmes suddenly leapt up and grabbed the side of the carriage for support.

'Driver!' he commanded. 'Stop a moment, please!'

Without a word, Holmes clambered down and strode off some fifty paces in front of us, looking this way and that. After which, he quickly returned to the carriage, and once again seated himself.

'And what was that all about?' I inquired.

Try as I might, I had not the slightest idea of the reason for his actions.

Holmes put a finger to his lips, a thoughtful look upon his face.

'I was merely observing,' he remarked, 'that while the obelisk can be perfectly viewed from here, or from the north, that it is completely hidden from view from the rest of the town by the church and mausoleum.'

'Which means?'

My friend shrugged. 'Perhaps nothing, Watson. And then, again ... very well, driver, carry on.'

As we lumbered forward, Holmes suddenly stood up again and peered intently at the high street ahead.

'What is that building?' he asked Blake. 'The one on the corner with the red shingle and trim?'

'That is Weatherby's inn,' the Doctor answered. 'Why do you ask?'

'Look for yourself,' Holmes replied. 'You will observe there is a crowd gathered in the street.'

'Perhaps you were right,' I told my friend. 'It seems to me we are expected.'

'I fear worse than that, Watson,' Holmes said grimly. 'I strongly suspect that the "Chilford Ripper" has struck again.'

FOUR

I felt decidedly uneasy as we alighted from our carriage. Before us stood a small crowd of locals, whose faces were clearly grim – and amongst them I observed Lestrade, engaged in conversation with a tall, dour-looking fellow. No sooner had we stepped down than a slim, flaxen-haired woman rushed to Doctor Blake's side, grabbing him by the arm.

'Geoffrey!' she cried. 'Oh, I am so glad you are back.' She glanced away. 'There has been another one...!'

'There, there, Gwen,' Blake comforted her. 'Under my roof, I am certain, you have nothing to fear.'

As they spoke, Lestrade and three others approached us.

'Why, Mr. Holmes, Doctor Watson! Whatever are you doing here?' Lestrade asked, pointedly. He looked sternly at the tall fellow at his side, who was eyeing us with some suspicion. 'Constable Newton informed me this very morning that we might well expect you, but still, I do admit, I am surprised.'

'I have been engaged by Doctor Blake,' Holmes replied, blandly. 'He seems to feel we might be of some assistance in this matter.'

Lestrade glanced around at the crowd that had gathered, then edged closer to us before speaking. I noted, as he drew Holmes aside, that instead of his usual condescending manner, there was a look of worry upon his lean, ferret-like face.

'To be frank, Mr. Holmes,' he said, lowering his voice so only we could hear, 'I welcome your help in this case, as we have worked well together in the past. It is, as I'm sure Constable Newton will agree, a very puzzling business.'

Holmes turned to the other three men.

'This is Doctor Watson,' he informed them, with a short wave of introduction. 'He is my closest associate, and can be trusted in any and all matters that might arise concerning this investigation.'

The tall man reached out and shook my hand heartily. The look of apprehension vanished from his face.

'I am Constable Newton,' he said, steadily. 'And these are two of our foremost citizens ... Mr. Weatherby, the innkeeper, and Stephen

Langley, owner of Briarwood Stables, of which I'm sure you have been told.'

At first glance, Weatherby seemed to me to be a decent sort, with a firm handshake and a ready smile. His cut-away shirt and rolled up sleeves bespoke of his profession, and his auburn hair was streaked with grey. Langley, attired in tan trousers and a dark Norfolk jacket, looked quite the country gentleman, a burly fellow with dark brown hair and wide shoulders, who must have weighed twelve stone. Though not as tall as Newton, his bull neck and thick sideboards gave a menacing look to his appearance.

'I am honoured, sir,' Langley said, as he shook our hands. 'I have no doubt that Geoffrey was wise to seek your assistance. If there is anything you require, do not hesitate to ask, and you may consider yourselves my guests at Langley Hall, for as long as is necessary.'

'Thank you,' Holmes replied, evenly, 'but Doctor Blake has already offered us the hospitality of his home. We shall be comfortable there, I am sure.' He turned to Lestrade, a grim look upon his face. 'By the remarks of Doctor Blake's fiancée, I deduce there has been another murder.'

'You are correct,' Lestrade replied, biting

out the words as though hating to admit it. 'The latest victim was Stanley Archer, the tobacconist. We found him not half an hour ago, in his quarters above the shop. By the condition of the body, I would say he was killed late last night, or quite early this morning. It appears the killer gained entry *via* the back stairs.'

'You have posted a guard, I presume,' Holmes asked, 'so that nothing has been disturbed?'

'I have,' the lean Inspector assured him. 'While our methods may differ, I am still appreciative of your habits. Shall we take a look, then?'

Holmes nodded his assent.

'An excellent suggestion,' he agreed. 'Although, I feel it best that only we four ... you, Newton, Watson and myself ... inspect the scene.' Holmes gave the others an apologetic look. 'Do not be offended, please,' he added, 'but it has been my experience that all too often valuable clues are destroyed when too many feet are trampling about the scene.'

Both Blake and the innkeeper acquiesced with a shrug, but Langley, I felt, seemed a little put out at not being included in our investigation.

'Very well,' he conceded, somewhat coldly. 'Such work, no doubt, is better left up to you. I shall be at the inn if you need me. And as I said, I am completely at your disposal.'

'Good man,' Newton said, slapping the fellow on the shoulder.

In his usual fashion, Lestrade quickly took the lead. 'Shall we go, then, gentlemen?' he said, with some authority. 'I suggest that we retrace the killer's steps, and enter Archer's lodgings from the alley.'

Moments later, we found ourselves at the backstairs that led to Stanley Archer's rooms, where a uniformed policeman stood guard.

'Watch your step, gentlemen,' Lestrade instructed, as we ascended to the rooms. 'As you can see, there is glass everywhere, especially in front of the door. That is, I deduce, how the killer gained entrance.' Carefully, Lestrade reached through a broken pane and opened the door. 'It would only take an instant to break the glass and slip the bolt like this, you see.'

Inside, the stench of death hung heavily in the air. During my years with Sherlock Holmes, I had borne witness to many grisly and sordid happenings, but still, I was hardly prepared for the horrible sight that awaited us.

Stanley Archer's mutilated body, clad only in a blood-stained cotton nightshirt, lay sprawled grotesquely upon the sunlit floor, his vacant eyes half open and his facial features waxen. His throat had been brutally slashed, causing an inordinate amount of blood to soak into the carpet, and from shoulder to spleen his body had been savagely stabbed and sliced by a series of gaping knife wounds that left his torso a sickening mesh of bloody cloth and flesh. Curiously, I noted, a small silk pillow and a revolver that lay but a few feet from the body.

Everything was a shambles. Sofa cushions were slashed, paintings on the wall hung askew, and the drawers of Archer's desk had been turned out and emptied, their contents strewn about the floor. The small kitchen table and chairs were also overturned, cupboard doors hung open, and even some dishes had been smashed. Shattered glass and scattered papers were upon the fire-place hearth, as well as a small tin dispatch box, whose twisted lid had obviously been prised open.

'Good Lord, Holmes!' I exclaimed. 'Blake

certainly did not exaggerate. This is a ghastly business. Look at the viciousness of those wounds. Why, I have seen nothing so appalling since Afghanistan.'

'Actually, it is a little reminiscent of Madame Carbono, the trunk murderess,' my friend replied, as he stepped carefully about, magnifying glass in hand. 'She had a grisly habit of dismembering her victims after she had poisoned them.' Holmes caught my puzzled look. 'It was before your time, Watson. Do those stairs from the kitchen lead down to the shop below, Constable?'

'Yes, sir, they do,' Newton replied. 'But I am a step ahead of you there. I have already examined the front door. It is locked and bolted from the inside, and nothing in the store seems out-of-place.'

'Has anyone else save Lestrade and you been through these rooms?'

'No, sir,' the Constable replied, firmly.

'Then how was the body discovered?'

'By one Meg Pryor, an employee at Weatherby's,' Lestrade interjected, again attempting to take the lead. It was clear to me, by the irked look on Newton's face, that a sort of rivalry had already developed here, between the obdurate local constable and the Scotland Yard inspector. Lestrade, it seemed, was determined to keep the upper hand.

Lestrade added, 'I am told by the good Constable that she and Archer had carried on a relationship for quite some time.'

'It was her habit,' Newton explained, with his local knowledge and some embarrassment, 'to fix him his bacon and eggs each morning, before he opened the store. She told us that when she saw the broken glass, she peered in and saw poor Archer lying there.' The Constable paused. 'As you might expect, she took it quite hard, sir. She's resting now in one of rooms at the inn.'

'An understandable reaction,' Holmes concurred. 'However, I shall still want to talk to her.'

Holmes knelt down beside the body, glancing about intently.

'The gun?' he questioned. 'Does it belong to Archer?'

'I am assuming so,' Newton declared. 'I do know that he owned one, and my search of his lodgings has produced no other weapon.'

Lestrade strode to Holmes' side.

'My theory,' he ventured, officiously, rubbing his chin, 'is that Archer came out of the bedroom, revolver in hand, when he heard the killer break the pane. There was a struggle, and his throat was slashed. After that, well, you can guess what happened next.'

The lean Constable glanced down at the mutilated corpse, then gave Holmes a disgusted look.

'I am not a man who frightens easily, Mr. Holmes,' he declared, solemnly. 'But it does give me some concern, thinking that the fiend who did this is walking in our midst.'

Holmes said nothing, but began to examine the body, first gently lifting up the back of Archer's head and then his blood-spattered right arm, peering underneath. After which, he crawled delicately back and forth about the room, his glass just inches from the floor. While we all looked on silently, Holmes returned to the kitchen, where he examined the overturned table and chairs, and pieces of one of the shattered dishes. At the fireplace, he picked up some shards of broken glass and put them under his lens. Then he strode to the cupboard and took out a clean bowl, scrutinising that as well. Newton, I observed, seemed somewhat perplexed by all this, while Lestrade and I, who were quite used to Holmes' unusual methods of investigation, took it in our stride.

'Well, sir,' Newton inquired, as Holmes rejoined us near the back door, 'have you discovered anything of interest? Something that might aid us in our investigation?'

Holmes gave the man a knowing look.

'You can cease looking for some sort of "Chilford Ripper" who broke in during the night,' he replied. 'Archer, I have no doubt, knew his killer. Well enough, in fact, that he turned his back upon him, which proved to be his fatal mistake.'

Lestrade could not hide his astonishment.

'Well, I never!' he exclaimed.

'I suspect that, like the others, Archer was rendered unconscious before he was killed. You may see for yourself. There is a bump on the back of his head as large as an egg.'

Lestrade gave Newton an inquiring glance. The Constable appeared uncomfortable and a not a little chagrined.

'I admire your thoroughness, sir,' he remarked to Holmes. 'I did miss that, I must admit.'

'Someone,' Holmes continued, 'has gone to considerable trouble to make not only this murder, but also the others, appear the work of a madman, and done quite a good job, I might add.'

'And how is that?' Lestrade asked. 'Why,

look about you! This vandalism, clearly, is not the work of any sane mind.'

Holmes shook his head. 'The facts speak otherwise, Lestrade. You said the murderer broke in through the backstairs door pane. Yet, if you look closely, you will observe there are only a few shards of glass on this side of the door. Almost all the glass is outside, on the stairway. Hence, the pane must have been broken from the inside...'

'By the killer, to simulate forced entry!' I interjected.

Holmes smiled. 'Exactly,' he said. 'Most likely after the deed was done. The killer showed up on a pretext, and Archer, in spite of the previous murders, trusted him enough to let him in. At some point, they decided to have a drink,' he conjectured, 'and when Archer turned to bring out the bottle, I suspect he was knocked unconscious. After which, he was dragged to the spot where he now lies. The pillow was placed upon his head to muffle any cries … and then the knife was brought into play.'

'And how do you deduce that?' Lestrade demanded, a hint of sarcasm in his voice.

Holmes gave him a faint smile.

'He was clearly lying senseless upon his back when the slaughter began,' Holmes stated. 'Look closely, and you will note that while there is blood everywhere, not a drop lies beneath him. Also, if you care to take my glass, you will see the path of Archer's heel marks indented in the carpet from here to there.'

Lestrade paused, but still did not appear convinced.

'But if, as you say, he knew the man, why did he draw his gun?'

'He did not. It was placed beside the body after the murder. A ploy, like the broken door pane, to throw you off the scent. The carpeting, you will note, is heavily splattered with blood. The gun, however, is clean.'

Lestrade spread his arms out wide and glanced about the dishevelled room with a look of exasperation.

'I see your logic as far as it goes, Mr. Holmes,' he said, 'but why all of this? Given what you've told us, it seems not only unnecessary, but senseless.'

'Because the rage of the "Chilford Ripper" is a ingenious mask, Lestrade, behind which our killer hides,' Holmes told him. 'It is a ruse of his own derivation, to insure that he could complete his crimes, and conceal something that he was seeking.'

'Complete?' Newton gasped. 'You expect

more murders, then?'

'I do, unless we can somehow unmask him first. The problem is, he has been so devilishly clever that we currently have no proof. At present, we are helpless, unless we catch him in the act.'

In spite of Holmes' assertions, one point continued to bother me.

'Still, the fact remains,' I insisted, 'that for whatever reason, the killer did ransack this room. Even if what you say is true, how could he destroy all this without waking someone from Weatherby's next door?'

'Quite easily,' Holmes confirmed. 'And I can show you how.'

He strode to the centre of the room.

'I ask you all to look around, and look closely. You will observe that while much is cut and slashed, and pictures hang askew, that nothing, save the whisky glass upon the fireplace and the door pane, is broken. I doubt that a mere tinkle of glass in the early hours would have roused anyone but the lightest sleeper.'

'Pardon me,' Newton interjected, 'but what about the overturned furniture? You are forgetting the kitchen.'

Holmes gave the tall policeman an amused look.

'Your choice of words hits the mark,' he said. 'For overturned, you see, is what they were. Had the table and chairs been knocked about in a struggle, or thrown over in a rage, you must admit there would be marks upon the edges, where they struck the floor. Yet when I examined them, the polish was remarkably undisturbed. Nor were there any marks to be found upon the floorboards.'

Grasping one of the overturned chairs, Holmes set it upright, then carefully turned it over and set it down again upon its side.

'That is how it was done,' he said. 'Did either of you hear a sound?'

'Wait a minute,' I inquired, pointing to the carpet. 'What about these china plates?'

'Were a lunatic throwing china or bric-a-brac about, I would expect to find shattered remnants everywhere,' Holmes replied. 'Instead we find four broken plates lying relatively close together and all are upon the carpet.'

Reaching into the cupboard, Holmes brought out three more plates, and laid them upside down in a row beside the others. Then, to our astonishment, he stepped upon the first, which shattered with a mild report, not unlike the sound of a cork being fired from a child's toy. Twice more, he ground his heel, producing the same result.

'The curvature of the plate towards the centre is, of course, its weakest point,' he observed. 'And the carpet muffles what little sound occurs. One other point! You will note that all the plates are lying face down. For a maniac throwing them to the floor, I find that miraculously consistent.'

Holmes then led us to the fireplace, where he lifted the small tin box from the hearth.

'Whether the killer found what he was looking for, I cannot say,' he admitted, ruefully. 'But I feel quite certain that it was prised open before the glass was smashed.' Noting my inquisitive look, he added, 'You see, when I first examined it, not merely the lid, but the interior as well, was covered with slivers.'

'I must admit, from what you say,' I remarked, 'that it all seems quite premeditated. Why, the only risk of discovery the killer took was when he smashed that glass and then broke the backdoor window.'

Newton scratched his head and frowned. 'So where do we go from here, Mr. Holmes?' he asked. 'Do you have a theory that you'd care to share?'

'I agree,' Lestrade added, pointedly. 'Given

all you have deduced, you must entertain some sort of explanation.'

'Not as yet,' my friend replied. 'But I will say that our killer is left handed.'

Lestrade frowned.

'And how do you know that?'

'From the location and angle of the wound to Archer's skull. I deduce that the killer was about the same height as his victim.' Holmes sighed, then motioned towards the door. 'Shall we? I think we have gleaned about all that is possible here.'

As we retraced our steps down the glass-strewn stairs, Newton paused and took Holmes' arm.

'I must admit, your assumptions do astound me,' he remarked, 'but upon reflection, they do seem to hold true.'

'If my assumptions are correct,' Holmes replied, 'then chances are fair that we shall have our killer this very night.'

'Tonight!' Lestrade gasped. 'Pardon me, but I think you are taking too much for granted.'

'Not so. Unless I am mistaken, our villain must strike at least once more, and I am hoping that you, Lestrade, will help to ensure that he makes that attempt before tomorrow.'

The Scotland Yard detective was clearly taken aback. 'Ensure he strikes again!' he exclaimed. 'I am not certain I want any part in that.'

'Ah, but you must,' Holmes insisted, 'if we are to corner this brute. There is no other way.'

Lestrade heaved a sigh. It seemed to me that he sensed he was indeed out of his depth, and had no choice but to agree to Holmes' suggestions.

'Very well, then,' he said, warily, 'what is it that you suggest?'

Holmes gave his associate a stern look.

'First, that you say nothing of our findings here,' he said. 'Only that, thanks to the investigative efforts of yourself and Constable Newton, we are now on the track of our killer, and should have confirmation of our theory tomorrow from London.' Holmes smiled. 'That should be enough to force our killer's hand, once the sun has set.'

'My goodness,' Newton murmured, 'and what do we do next?'

Holmes did not immediately reply. The reflective look on his lean face told me that his mind was, at that particular moment, racing furiously ahead, exploring and eliminating any number of untold possibilities we might face.

'There are three people to whom I particularly wish to speak,' he replied, at length. 'Meg Pryor, of course, Langley and Gwendolyn Tate.'

'Gwen Tate?' the Constable echoed back. 'The other two I can understand. Langley was a close friend of Archer's, and Meg knew him intimately, but whatever could Gwen Tate have to do with this?'

'According to Doctor Blake, she was Molly Brighton's closest friend,' Holmes explained. 'I am convinced that her murder occurred for a different reason than the others, and I am hopeful that she can shed some light on why. Following those interviews, I shall pay a visit to the industrious Edward Lattimer and draft my telegram to London.'

'But whatever for?' Lestrade demanded. 'I am here. You should need no further assistance.'

'True, to a certain extent,' Holmes told him, 'but, to be candid, I still need to seek confirmation of certain facts.'

I could see, as we walked back through the alley, that while Lestrade appeared uncomfortable by this turn of events, he was unwilling to confront the logic of Holmes' deductions. Newton, however, seemed unperturbed, recognising I felt, the depth of my companion's superior intellect.

'Locating the three you mentioned should not be difficult,' he said, as we turned the corner onto the street. 'My guess is that we'll find them all at the inn.'

Once inside, we espied Langley at the bar, a glass in hand. He immediately rushed over to us.

'So, gentlemen,' he asked eagerly, 'what progress have you made in this sordid business?'

Lestrade hooked his thumbs in his lapels, and gave the horseman his most officious Scotland Yard look.

'I can only say that, after examining the scene, new facts have come to light,' he stated, quite loud enough for anyone close by to hear. 'I cannot go into details, of course, but I will telegraph London for some particulars and by tomorrow I feel confident that we will be ready to close the net. Three additional constables will arrive on the morning train.'

Langley took a sip from his glass.

'If it is manpower for a search you need,' he said, 'I can be of help there. I've half a dozen good fellows we can send through the fields. And I shall be glad to join in myself, if need be.'

'Assistance from a military man is always welcome,' Holmes stated evenly. 'Who knows? We may require another hand. Oh, by the way, Doctor Blake was telling us of your unique club as we journeyed here this morning. I must commend you upon your dedication to a fallen comrade. What was your regiment again?'

'The Essex Guards,' Langley said. 'I was a Quartermaster.'

'Ah, yes. I had forgotten that. But that is peculiar. I was not aware that the Essex Guards were stationed in Bombay.'

Langley smiled thinly.

'There is no mystery there,' he said, 'only a slight misunderstanding by Blake, which I can easily correct. Yes, I was in Bombay for a short time, but with the 56th Berkshires. However, I would hardly call them my regiment. I was only transferred there shortly before I was discharged, to temporarily fill a vacancy. I had just about enough time to unpack, before I was ordered home.'

'I see. And how long were you attached to the Berkshires?'

I caught a glint of stiffening in Langley's eyes.

'Why, a month or two, I suppose. I cannot

recall exactly.'

'No matter, it is of no importance,' Holmes insisted, dismissing the subject with a wave of his hand. 'A curiosity, only. And you were discharged in...'

'Ninety-one,' the horseman said. I thought I detected a hint of irritation in his voice.

Holmes gave the man a bland smile. 'At which time, Doctor Blake informed us, you returned to Briarwood in the autumn. Please accept my condolences, sir, upon the loss of your father while you so ably served the Queen. But having met you, I feel certain that you are a highly resourceful fellow and that Briarwood remains in steady hands.'

As Langley emptied his glass, I noticed a brief look of displeasure on his face.

'Your compliment is appreciated,' the big man remarked. 'I can assure you, managing a stable of our size and reputation is no easy task. It requires a great deal of both fore-sight and time. Given that, if you have no more questions, I shall be on my way. If I seem abrupt, it is because I am offended by your repeated refusal of my help. I have already lost two friends to this killer and I do not wish to lose another.'

For a second, Langley cast Holmes a stony gaze, then turned and walked away.

'I do not care for that man, Holmes,' I said in a low voice. 'I cannot put my finger on it, but I do not care for him at all.'

'Nor do I, Watson. But, you must admit, his point is well taken. Should our circumstances be reversed I would probably act in a similar manner.'

From across the room, Constable Newton approached us.

'Meg Pryor is still resting upstairs,' he told us. 'Blake insists she is in somewhat of a fragile state. But to my mind, she seems improved enough to answer questions.'

'And Gwendolyn Tate?'

'She is, Blake told me, currently visiting Mrs. McVey.'

'I see. Well, then, I shall see them both once this interview is concluded. Who knows? Mrs. McVey may be of help as well.'

Moments later, we were all standing outside Meg Pryor's door, which Newton tapped upon lightly.

'Who is it?' we heard Blake call.

'Newton and Lestrade,' the Constable replied, 'with Sherlock Holmes and Doctor Watson.'

'Very well. Come in.'

Seldom have I seen a more forlorn countenance than that of the sorrowful woman we beheld as we entered the room, propped up by pillows upon the bed. Beneath her long auburn tresses, her tear-streaked face was strained and pale, and her dark brown eyes looked up at us beseechingly in a hopeless sort of way.

Blake patted her hand reassuringly.

'Mr. Holmes and Doctor Watson have come up from London,' he said, softly. 'They are detectives, who are here to render their assistance.'

At the utterance of Blake's words, the woman suddenly began to sob, her shoulders shaking.

'And of what good is that?' she asked, between her gasps. 'My Arch is gone. He's gone forever. Nothing else much matters now.'

'What matters, missy,' Newton stated, 'is that we apprehend this murderer. I realise, for you, that Archer's death has been a horrible shock, but Mr. Holmes needs to ask a few pertinent questions. Time is not on our side, Meg. Even in your sorrow, you must think of the other locals as well. We have suspicions that this killer will soon strike again.'

Newton's earnest words seemed to shake the woman from her reverie. Looking up at us again, she hastily wiped the tears from her pale cheeks.

'You must understand,' she moaned, 'we were talking of marriage in the spring. I know I am not an attractive catch, but Arch always made me feel like a queen. He was a good man. My chance for happiness, and now, what prospects do I have? Not much, I'd say, in this remote town. I shall, I fear, spend my remaining years alone.'

I could detect an urgency in Holmes' expression. There were questions, I knew, he wished to ask. Yet he paused for a moment, out of respect for the poor woman's plight.

'Had anything been bothering Archer recently?' he inquired, at length. 'Had he changed his habits in any way?'

The woman looked at him with some surprise.

'However did you know?' she asked. 'His recent manner, had in fact, begun to worry me dreadfully.' She began to sob again. 'Deep down,' she said, 'I feared it would come to this.'

Holmes, I could see, was somewhat irritated by the woman's second outburst. He was, after all, a person who put little stock in female emotions. His was the world of keen observation and calculated deduction, and having discovered what he felt was an important clue, I had no doubt he would pursue it doggedly regardless of her feelings.

'And when did this change in his nature occur?' Holmes persisted, calmly, lighting a cigarette.

After a glance at Blake, Meg Pryor composed herself, and straightened up in the bed.

'It was the morning they discovered Harper's body,' she replied. 'We had just opened the shop, when a boy ran in and told us what had happened. The news, I could tell, affected Arch greatly. The colour simply drained from his face. For a time, he said nothing, but just stared out of the shopfront window into the street. It was clear that he was mulling something over ... something that had gripped him fiercely.'

'Perhaps it was merely the shock of losing a close friend,' I suggested. 'I have known that to happen in such cases.'

Meg Pryor shook her head. 'No,' she insisted, 'there was more to it than that. After a while, a steely look came into his eyes, and his whole face seemed to stiffen up, you know? But when I asked him what was on his mind, he refused to say.'

'And then?' Holmes pressed.

The woman's grip tightened upon her covers.

'He then did something that was extremely strange,' she told us. 'He walked behind the counter, took out his revolver and tucked it inside his belt.'

'And why did that surprise you?' I interjected. 'It seems a common enough response to me.'

'Because, from the day I'd known him, Arch had an aversion to that piece,' she replied. 'It had something to do with his time in the services, though I hardly know the details. But I do know one thing ... only the most dire circumstances would have caused him to bring it out.' She heaved a sigh. 'And yet, from that moment on, it was always on his person or close at hand, day and night.'

'Perhaps it was a mere precaution,' Holmes told her. 'Or did he indicate he felt personally threatened in some way?'

'He never said as much, but that is my belief,' the woman answered. 'During the day, I noticed, he never ventured far from the shop, and our nightly walks were altered drastically.'

'Your nightly walks?' Holmes echoed. 'How so?'

'It had always been our habit, unless the weather was inclement, to take a stroll in the evening. It was our talking time, while we took in the fields and the sky. Arch loved the stars. Why, he could pick out the various constellations in an instant. But after Harper's death, we never took to the fields again. Arch insisted we only walk about the village and never further than the bridge across the stream.' She smiled faintly. 'But, perhaps you are right. Perhaps he was only worried about my safety.'

'What did he talk about on these short-ened walks?' Holmes inquired. 'Did he give any hint of what was troubling him?'

'Never,' she replied. 'But he did tell me that he planned to leave the village soon. "Our future is not here," he said. "Not if we are to be happy. There is one matter I must address, and then we shall leave this place for good."'

Holmes seemed surprised.

'Indeed? By what I was told, the members of The Cooper Club have all prospered since they took up residence here, and were all quite content.'

'Arch was before,' she declared, 'but not after Harper's death. I know, because of what I heard, the night I followed him.'

'You followed him? When was that?'

'The night after Harper's death,' the woman recalled. 'The night poor old Toby got the knife. Arch insisted we only walk the lighted streets, as I said. But when we reached the bridge, he again did something strange. He glanced at his watch, and then instead of walking me back to the inn, he sent me off with a kiss. "I shall see you in morning," he said. "I have an errand to run".

'"An errand?" I cried. "At this hour? Arch, you tell me now! What is this all about?"

'"Not to worry," he insisted. "Men's business ... off with you now!"

'So I did as he instructed and walked back across the street, but once I reached the corner I turned back and followed him from a distance.'

Holmes' eyes gleamed with anticipation.

'And where did he go?' my friend asked. 'And pray, what did you see?'

'Arch turned in at the cemetery gate,' Meg Pryor said. 'He strode off through the grave-yard, the revolver in his hand, and met two others beside the big obelisk on the other side.'

'Indeed! And who were they?'

'I cannot tell you. The moon, you see, was hardly full and I could approach no closer without the risk of being discovered. At any rate, once Arch had arrived, they began to talk.'

'Could you identify their voices?'

'No, I could only hear murmurs, I was so far away But they were angry murmurs, I'll swear to that. The only words I recognised were Arch's at the end. "Hang, how you do it!" he yelled. "All I know is I want out! I want my share, and now!" And then he stormed back towards the gate, where I was standing.'

'It was only then I realised my plight. If I returned back up the road, he would surely see me. So I tried to hide beside the fence, but it was no good. He spotted me as he walked past, grabbed me by the shoulders and pulled me to my feet.'

'"What are you doing, following me?" he asked, angrily, "and how much did you hear?"

'"I heard nothing, Arch," I told him. "I swear it – on our love I swear." He pulled me to him and hugged me hard. "Thank God," he said, fiercely. "Because the less you know, the better." Then he lifted up my chin, and gave me a reassuring look. "This will all be over soon," he said, "and then we're gone. I promise. Come on, I shall walk you back, as

I should have done before."

'When we reached the inn, Arch bade me to sit a moment upon the bench. "I have thought it over," he told me, "and I cannot lie to you. I feel a dangerous game is being played, and I am not sure how it will end. But I do want to look out for you. Just remember, Meg, if anything happens to me, go and check my soldier's pockets. There is a document inside that will make you rich. But for now, you must not, cannot, say a word to anyone."'

She uttered another sob. 'And now,' she said, tearfully, 'it has.'

Holmes appeared struck.

'But, of course,' he cried. 'The painting!'

In a flash, Holmes leaped up and bounded from the room, leaving the rest of us no choice but to follow. Down the alley and up the glass-strewn stairs we went, where we found my friend standing before Stanley Archer's blood-stained couch, holding a large painting of a British subaltern in his hands.

'Alas, we are too late,' he informed us, a disappointed look upon his face. 'Our killer is not only clever, but quite fortunate. I doubt he would have found what was hidden here, had he not first slashed the painting from the front.'

'What do you mean?' Newton asked.

Holmes turned the painting over to reveal a small neat slice in the canvas backing.

'How else could he have discovered it?' he asked, dejectedly.

'And what do you think he found?' I inquired.

Holmes frowned. 'A document, I suspect, that would have sent our killer to the gallows,' he said, as he put the canvas down, 'and, quite likely, have earned Meg Pryor a substantial reward. How unfortunate. Had it still been in its place, we would have had the proof we needed to snare our man.'

'Mr. Holmes,' Newton observed, with some frustration, 'you are apparently far ahead of me in this. I would appreciate an explanation.'

'And I, as well,' Lestrade demanded. 'Come now, inform us of your theory.'

'Not until I have verified my facts by telegraphing London,' Holmes replied. 'For now, I have only suspicions but no evidence to prove my case.'

We retraced our steps to the inn where Holmes surprised me by returning to Meg Pryor's room, where Blake was dispensing a sedative.

'My apologies for my abrupt departure,' he told the woman. 'You have my deepest sympathies. I have no doubt that Stanley Archer's actions were only for your protection. It seems clear that he cared for you a great deal. If it helps at all, know that your information has aided us immensely.'

Meg Pryor drew herself up, and looked Holmes in the eye.

'If you can find the fiend who did my Arch,' she told him, 'I shall be eternally grateful. I only hope I can be there to watch the day that he swings.'

'You rest now,' Blake told her. 'I shall call back and look in later this afternoon.'

As we descended the stairs, Holmes turned to Blake.

'There are some questions I should like to ask your fiancée,' he told him. 'I was told she was visiting Mrs. McVey.'

Blake seemed startled. 'And what has Gwen to do with all of this?' he demanded.

'Calm yourself, Doctor. I merely feel, as Molly Brighton's friend, she may be able to shed some light on matters.'

'Very well,' the other replied. 'I shall take you there myself.'

'That won't be necessary,' I observed, as we stepped into the street. 'Unless I am mistaken, that is her returning across the bridge.'

In moments, Miss Tate was at our side.

'And how was Mrs. McVey?' Blake asked. 'We were about to join you both.'

Gwendolyn Tate gave him a frown.

'Stubborn,' she replied. 'I had hoped she would move in with us, until the killer was apprehended. But she would have none of it. "My doors are locked, and I have Arthur's shotgun," she told me. "Thank you, I shall be fine."' Miss Tate gave her husband-to-be a pleading glance. 'Geoffrey, would you see her, please? She may be proud, but she is also old and all alone. Perhaps you can convince her otherwise.'

'Your reasoning is sound, my dear,' Blake agreed. 'We shall pay another call, presently. Oh! But first Mr. Holmes has a few questions he would like to ask, concerning Molly Brighton. I told him you would not mind.'

A veil of sadness fell over Miss Tate's face, at the mention of her late friend's name.

'For Molly's sake, I shall do whatever I can,' she said, determinedly.

'For that, please accept my sincere gratitude,' Holmes declared. 'Doctor Blake told us that you were Molly's closest friend. Given that, I would imagine you shared much together.'

A look of hesitation came into Miss Tate's eyes.

'Such as?'

'Her husband. How did he die?'

'Gordon drowned three years ago, in a sailing accident off Clacton.'

'I see. And how did it happen? Are you aware of the details?'

'It was a rough day, Molly told me, but he insisted on going out. Somehow, he lost his balance and fell overboard and went under before anyone could reach him.'

'Ah, he was alone then?'

'No. He was sailing with Stephen Langley.'

Holmes and I exchanged a glance.

'I see. And after his death, did your friend still wear her wedding ring? I am told that widows often do, out of respect.'

'She has worn it ever since the first day I met her,' Miss Tate replied. A curious look came upon her face. 'That is, until a few days ago. It was the day she died, to be exact.'

'Surely, that must have seemed unusual to you,' Holmes remarked. 'Did you inquire as to why?'

For a moment, Miss Tate hesitated.

'Go on, Gwen,' Blake interjected. 'This is not a time to hold things back.'

'And I do not mean to,' Miss Tate explained, sadly. 'It's only that ... well, she was so happy that day. Who could have guessed she would never see another?'

The woman took a handkerchief from her sleeve, dabbing moisture from her eyes before continuing.

'It was about four in the afternoon,' she recalled. 'I had stopped in to see Molly on another matter. Well, the moment I walked inside, I could tell she was absolutely brimming. It was, as we sat down, that I noticed her bare finger. "Molly," I asked, "wherever is your ring?" "Gone for good," she said, in a whisper, "but there will be another to replace it soon." As you can imagine, I was overjoyed for her. Her eyes were dancing and her face just glowed. "I have a new acquaintance," she continued, "a fellow I know will take good care of me. He has already mentioned marriage."'

Holmes whistled.

'And who was this unknown admirer?' he asked. 'This person who offered such expectations?'

Miss Tate frowned again.

'That was the curious part,' she admitted. 'No matter how I formed my plea, she would not reveal his identity. "He has asked for time, and I shall give it to him," she told me. "I am trusting you to keep my confidence. If I tell you now, it will put a Jonah on me for sure."' Miss Tate paused. 'I am sure you understand,' she added, 'why, as a friend, I could not pursue the matter further. While I was hurt by her refusal, I knew she must have her reasons and would reveal her suitor to me in her own good time.'

'But surely,' Holmes persisted, 'you must have some idea as to the identity of this man? Chilford is, after all, a small community where even the mildest flirtations are unlikely to go unnoticed. Is there anyone you can think of who had shown an interest in Molly of late?'

'Not of a serious nature. Oh, there are half a dozen young men in the area ... farmhands, mostly. True, some are quite strong and handsome, but Molly was no trollop. She knew their expectations, and would not have given them the time of day.'

Holmes gave her a penetrating look.

'What about others then? Harper? Hastings? Or Stephen Langley, perhaps...?'

Miss Tate pulled a face.

'The devil would have had Molly's bed before Thomas Harper,' she declared, flatly.

'The man, to put it directly, was lecherous. Molly told me more than once, if you wore skirts and still had your own teeth, he would always be there asking.'

'And Hastings?'

'Perhaps. He is local and has no reputation. And, now that I think of it, his farm is quite secluded.'

'And Langley...?'

'I know the two were friendly,' the woman stated, 'but I never saw indications it was anything more than that. I do recall Stephen inquiring once about how Molly was managing financially. I think he has always harboured guilt, concerning Gordon's death.'

'That he was not able to rescue him?' I asked.

'Yes.'

Holmes threw up his hands in sheer frustration.

'But who then, was it,' he cried, 'who so captured her affections?'

'My theory,' Blake's fiancée ventured, 'is that it was a gentleman, a professional person, if you will, and not from our town. Colchester, perhaps? Why, even Mersea is but a few miles away.' She paused a moment, then added, 'I base this theory on another remark she made, during our last conversation.'

'Indeed?'

'Yes. "Much as I loved Gordon," she told me, "things shall be different this time around. No more farmer's life for me. This time, I shall be able to sleep in late, and have tea brought to me in bed..."'

Tears welled again in Miss Tate's eyes.

'That is what makes this all so awful,' she said. 'Because, it seemed, that Molly was on the verge of finding her dreams, the happiness and security that she so wanted. I shall never forget her last words to me, as I left the cottage. "God's oath now, Gwen, don't you breathe a word," she implored me. "For this is so important to me, as you will, in time, come to realise."

'"But of course," I told her. "There is no doubt you are quite happy." Then she gave me a fierce hug, and said, "Count on it, my dear. It won't be long before I am sleeping in late. And when I have that ring, you shall be the first to know."'

Miss Tate's shoulders began to shake.

'And now,' she sobbed, 'she's dead...'

Blake pulled his fiancée to him, rested her head upon his shoulder and gave my companion an angry look.

'Unless you have any other important questions...' he began.

'None whatsoever,' Holmes replied. 'Miss Tate, I do apologise for the dreadful inconvenience. If it is any consolation, know that you have been a great help in all of this.'

The woman looked up at Holmes. 'It has been painful, I do admit,' she said. 'But if it will help catch Molly's killer, I would undergo it all again.'

'You are, I can see, made of the sternest fibre,' Holmes told her. 'Given his profession, I feel Doctor Blake is fortunate to have a companion such as you. And Molly could not have asked for a better friend.'

'These are trying times for all of us,' Blake said. 'Molly, I suggest we cross the stream, so that I may speak with Mrs. McVey.' The Doctor paused, then added, 'You gentlemen are all welcome to the house for a late lunch, perhaps. How does three o'clock suit you?'

'A gracious invitation, but I must refuse,' Newton replied. 'Given the observations of Mr. Holmes, I wish to inspect Archer's flat again, before the body is removed. Lestrade?'

There was a challenge in Newton's tone, and Lestrade could not resist the bait.

'I shall accompany you, of course,' the policeman replied. He gave my companion a wry look. 'Mr. Holmes is quite thorough.

But perhaps we shall find something that he has missed.'

Newton frowned. 'You mentioned,' he said to Holmes, 'that you wanted to speak with Lattimer, the undertaker.'

'I do, as soon as possible,' my friend replied.

The Constable stretched out his arm. 'That is his establishment there,' the policeman said, 'on the corner opposite Weatherby's.'

'I noted that when we arrived. But will he be there? Perhaps we would have more luck if we accompany you to the murder scene.'

'I guarantee, you will not find Edward Lattimer there,' Newton said, dryly.

'And why is that?'

'Because I have not sent for him,' the Constable explained. 'Time is money to that man. He will not appear, until he receives my summons and is thus permitted to charge expenses.'

'Perhaps he is simply a sound businessman,' I remarked. 'You make him out to be quite the miser.'

'As well I should,' Newton replied, gruffly. 'I have lived in this town all my life, Doctor Watson. And in that time I have not witnessed or heard of one example of the man's generosity. He is as tight-fisted as a Scotsman.'

With that, the Constable turned on his heel and walked away with Lestrade at his side.

'I seem to have touched upon a sore spot with our friend Newton,' Holmes commented, with a slight smile. 'It seems quite clear, he does not care much for Mr. Lattimer, or his motives. Ah, well, come along Watson. I must see him immediately, in any case.'

'Can we expect you for lunch?' Blake inquired. 'Or shall your duties keep you elsewhere as well?'

Holmes smiled. 'Watson will, I am certain, need some sustenance for the fields,' Holmes remarked. 'For my part, a fresh pipe will do. Once having sent my telegram to London, I should like to examine the scenes of the previous murders, although, I suspect, by this time, there are few clues left to glean.'

'I must admit, Holmes,' I said, as we made our way back up the street, 'you have made me feel like some sort of lazybones. The blasted hunting can wait. My place is to be beside you.'

Holmes stopped and re-lit his pipe, whose smoke was instantly swept away by the sunny afternoon breeze.

'Our cause can be better helped if you keep your engagement,' my friend replied. 'While I am playing out my theory, I want you to observe as much as you can about Geoffrey Blake, his house and habits. While my instincts tell me one thing, I still cannot be certain of his role in all of this.'

My friend's remarks stirred me to the quick.

'Surely, you don't think Blake is somehow connected with these murders?' I expostulated. 'That, I simply cannot believe.'

'And yet he is, Watson,' Holmes insisted, 'although he, himself, may not know it. It is my fervent hope that he is merely a pawn, and nothing more.'

'A pawn? For whom? Whatever do you mean?'

Holmes gave me a knowing glance.

'One thing I did not tell the constabulary, Watson, was that I observed traces of whisky upon the shards of glass in Archer's flat. A bottle remained in the kitchen cupboard half empty, but intact.'

'I do see a connection,' I admitted. 'Blake said there was a bottle found in Harper's rooms as well. But how can you put so much into a trifle?'

A weary look crossed Holmes' face.

'Because,' he said, 'it is a very telling clue and one, as a military man, I am surprised you failed to recognise.'

I could not hide my exasperation.

'And that is?'

'After murdering both Harper and Archer,' Holmes explained, 'the murderer poured himself a drink, but not for the lack of nerve, as I first suspected. No. He was carrying out an old tradition before he began his grisly work. A toast, Watson. A final toast to a departed comrade.'

It was as if a curtain had been lifted before my eyes.

'But, of course!' I cried. 'Why, there must have been some sort of cabal here, amongst these ex-servicemen. That certainly would explain Archer's demand for "his share" at the cemetery. Wait a moment, though! That does not explain the death of Toby Turner, or poor Molly Brighton.'

Holmes patted me on the shoulder as we proceeded.

'Your points are well taken,' he remarked, ruefully, as he puffed upon his clay. 'But trust me, there is a connection. The Brighton woman's murder, I feel certain, has something to do with her mysterious suitor.'

'And Turner's death?'

'At this point, I have not a clue,' Holmes admitted. 'It may be something as simple as happenstance or something as complicated as subterfuge. But come! I must get my telegram off to London. My entire theory rests upon Mycroft's reply to my inquiries.'

As we walked up the street, my mind continued to cogitate upon the unlikely group called The Cooper Club and what devilish reasons might lie behind its original creation.

'But if what you say is true, then a rift has surely arisen amongst these soldiers,' I observed. 'And a deadly one, at that. Two of them have been murdered, after all. Have you any idea what this connection might entail?'

'A conspiracy of the highest order, Watson,' my friend replied. 'And yet, at this moment, I have not one shred of evidence that could bring our man before the courts.' We paused before the undertakers. 'But if my surmises are correct, we have stumbled upon the answer to one of the greatest and most well-concealed crimes of the decade.'

FIVE

Lattimer's shop appeared deserted. The full length curtains were drawn shut and the door, we found, was locked. As Holmes gave the bell a ring, I could not help but notice the hand-lettered sign that had been placed against the glass, which read:

TELEGRAM OFFICE
REGISTRAR
SMALL COMMISSIONS
UNDERTAKEN

'What a cheery place,' I remarked, sarcastically, 'although I suppose one must expect that from a undertaker. Nobody seems at home, at any rate.'

Holmes gave the bell another ring, and then another. Suddenly, the door swung open a crack, and we were confronted by a small, bespectacled man with a weathered face, a balding pate, and sidewhiskers as white as snow. In his right hand, he held a large revolver.

'And who are you?' he asked, suspiciously.

'Do not be alarmed, Mr. Lattimer,' Holmes assured him. 'I am Sherlock Holmes, and this is Doctor Watson, my associate. We are here at the behest of Doctor Blake and Constable Newton, to try and put an end to these horrible murders, of which, I feel certain, you are already aware there has been another.'

The small man arched an eyebrow.

'I suspected as much,' he said. 'Weatherby, was it, this time?'

'And why would you think that?' Holmes asked.

'My vision is no way impaired, sir. I saw the crowd gathered outside the inn.'

'Ah, you did not inquire, then? You were not the least bit curious?'

'I am a man who keeps to his own affairs,' the fellow replied. 'Given the type of services I offer, people generally come to me.'

'And that is why we are here,' Holmes explained. 'Might we come inside? There is an urgent telegram I wish to send at once to London.'

'Why, but, of course!' the small man declared, obviously pleased that he had a customer at hand. He swung the door open and beckoned us to enter.

'So, if not Weatherby, who was it then?'

Lattimer inquired, as we crossed to the front counter.

'The latest victim was Stanley Archer, the tobacconist,' I informed him. 'He was found in the flat above his store.'

'Archer, you say?!' The little man cried. He issued a caustic laugh. 'Well, I can tell you one thing for sure. His passing will have the regulars crying in their beer, come closing time. They had become accustomed to the man's largesse.' Lattimer shuddered. 'A grotesque business, this,' he added, almost to himself. 'I expect I shall be receiving another summons from Newton soon.'

Darting behind the counter, the wiry fellow put down the revolver, brought out a pad and pencil, and offered them to my friend. 'My apologies for this,' he said, motioning towards the gun, 'but given all that's happened here, one cannot be too cautious.'

'No offence is taken, I assure you,' Holmes replied. 'I take it, however, you do not share much confidence in Constable Newton's capabilities.'

'If he had any, would Scotland Yard be here? Would you be here?' Lattimer asked, snapping out the words. 'If he had any, would four of our locals now be dead? And each cut up like a joint for Sunday dinner, before the last one's cold.' Lattimer slapped his hand upon the counter with agitation. 'And what has Newton discovered? Nothing!'

'Your frustrations are quite understandable,' Holmes answered, coolly. 'But I feel your judgment of Newton to be unduly harsh. This matter, I can say with some certainty, goes far deeper than anyone here could fathom. You may be thankful that Blake and Newton asked for our assistance.'

'I shall be thankful,' Lattimer declared, heatedly, 'when this killer has been apprehended and not before.'

'Then to that end,' Holmes said, 'I shall compose my telegram. If you will pardon me?' Taking up pad and pencil, he turned on his heel and moved to a nearby table, where he began scribbling furiously.

'I could not help but notice your sign outside,' I mentioned, as we waited for Holmes to finish. 'Doctor Blake told us you were quite an industrious fellow. Undertaker, telegraphist, registrar, groundsman ... you have a hand, it seems, in many things.'

'A man has to do what he can to make a decent living,' the undertaker replied defensively. 'My father taught me early in life to never be afraid of work. And there are no two ways about it, Doctor, it is the early bird who gets the worm.' The little man puffed out his chest with pride. 'I can tell you one thing, they'll not have to hold a charity day for me.'

'Of that, sir, I feel quite certain,' I agreed, with some chagrin.

At that moment, the door of Lattimer's shop swung open, and a tall young fellow with reddish hair stepped inside.

'I am here on behalf of Constable Newton,' he said, officiously. 'There has been another murder, and we require your assistance.'

'And you shall have it, Hansen,' Lattimer replied, gruffly, 'when I have finished my business here. Outside of some fluid and a decent coffin, there is little I can do for Stanley Archer now. Tell Newton I shall been along directly.'

'Yes, sir,' the young man said stiffly, unable to hide his displeasure. Without another word, he turned and left the same way he had come, slamming the door behind him.

For another few minutes, Holmes continued with his telegram. When he finally rose and handed it to Lattimer, the undertaker looked astonished.

'Are you certain you wish me to send all this?' he asked, glancing at the pages. 'It is, after all, quite a lengthy message. The charge, you should know, is two shillings for the first fifty words, and a ha'penny a word after that.'

'The charge is of no concern,' Sherlock Holmes assured him. 'In fact, I can guarantee you that if this telegram bears fruit it will be worth a thousand times the cost. And you, sir, will be able to once again unlock your doors, and put your revolver away.'

Lattimer's eyes widened in awe, almost like a child on Christmas morning.

'You don't say?'

'I do. And I trust that you will keep the contents of this telegram, and its reply, strictly in your confidence.' Holmes gave the telegraphist a withering look. 'You must understand,' he said, his voice rising, 'this is not a matter of who killed someone's sheep. Government issues are at stake. Should you compromise our investigation, I can assure you I shall see you standing in the dock facing charges, no less, of abetting a conspiracy, and perhaps even treason!'

Lattimer swallowed hard. Holmes' remarks, it seemed abundantly clear, had made the desired impression.

'Oh, you can trust me, sir!' he declared, his voice quaking. 'Not a word of this shall pass my lips. Why, until you spoke, I had no idea of the implications. The last thing I would want to do is hamper a Government investigation!'

Holmes smiled evenly.

'Then to that end,' he continued, 'I am sure you wouldn't mind answering a question or two while I am here. For there are certain local matters of interest, which you, in your official and *ex-officio* capacities, presumably have some knowledge.'

'Why, why of course, sir,' Lattimer stammered. 'I shall be more than glad to help, if I can.'

Holmes reached for a match, and deliberately let the fellow stew for another moment or two while he re-lit his clay.

'Now, then. As Registrar, would you know how many horses have been bought and sold by Briarwood Stables over the past three years?'

Lattimer gave my friend a sly look.

'As Registrar, I would have no idea,' he proclaimed. 'But as a well-informed citizen, shall we say, I know for a fact that two of his best thoroughbreds, *Whistler's Fancy* and *Brandywine*, were sold recently. The *Whistler* went a year ago last April, and *Brandywine* this spring. Both have since shown their colours and finished well in the Derby ... there can be no doubt about their bloodlines.'

'I see. And have there been any major additions in recent months?'

The little man smiled, knowingly.

'Not to my knowledge,' he answered, 'in my official capacity.'

'And unofficially...?'

'As a well-informed citizen,' Lattimer continued, 'I should also tell you there are some who say Stephen Langley's real penchant is betting on the thoroughbreds, rather than breeding them. He has, it's rumoured, taken out some heavy loans of late.'

'Loans, you say?'

'Not I. Although I am sure a certain bank in Colchester could confirm it.'

'And that firm would be?' Holmes asked, intently.

'The Mercantile Bank would be my guess. They have handled the family's interests for years.'

Holmes reached again for the pencil and paper, and quickly scribbled some lines. 'An addendum to my telegram,' he explained, as he handed over the sheet. 'And so you feel that Briarwood's future is somewhat clouded?'

'All I will say is that Langley is not the horseman his father was.'

'And why is that?'

'Because Sir Harold would never have sold his two best stallions without promising foals to take their place.'

Holmes, I could see, was impressed.

'No foals, you say? My, my. Then it does seem the stable, shall we say, is currently resting upon its laurels?'

'Current enough to those who know the business,' Lattimer replied, with a wink. 'The truth is, his younger mounts have yet to claim a major trophy. Insiders will tell you the best of the lines are gone and that he must re-invest soon or face ruin.'

'How interesting,' Holmes observed. 'But to know all this, I take it you must be an insider of sorts yourself. Do you follow the horses, then?'

'Only from a distance,' Lattimer answered, 'and strictly as a hobbyist. Shillings are too hard to come by, sir, to risk in games of chance. And for that reason, gambling has never held any attraction for me.'

For a moment, Holmes said nothing more, content to draw upon his pipe.

'There is one other matter,' he remarked, at length. 'When Langley and his friends returned from India, they brought back the body of Harry Cooper, a comrade, Blake told us, who had been killed in action overseas. Do you recall, precisely, what was the cause of death?'

Lattimer shrugged his shoulders.

'According to the paperwork I was given, he died of a gunshot wound,' he recalled. 'The truth is, however, I never saw the body.'

Holmes seemed astonished.

'But as the town undertaker,' he insisted. 'Was it not you who handled the arrangements?'

'Only in a fashion, sir. Actually, there was little for me to do. According to the paperwork, the lad had been embalmed; the body arrived in a coffin that had already been provided. My services consisted of simply securing a grave and the obelisk ... and the actual burial, of course.' Lattimer stroked his chin and frowned. 'It was not, I must tell you, a very profitable business, once the diggers had been paid.'

'And who chose the location of the grave?' Holmes asked.

'Why, they all did, sir. Although, now that I recall, it was quite a convoluted procedure. We must have wandered about the grounds for nearly an hour, before a decision was finally made.'

'Indeed,' I commented. 'And why was that?'

'Why, because they had differing opinions on exactly where the lad's box should go. Harper favoured a shady spot I showed them at the far end of the cemetery, next to the woods. Hastings wanted a plot located close to the road. Archer, on the other hand...'

Holmes interrupted him with a wave of his hand.

'And what about Langley?' he asked. 'Where did he prefer that Harry Cooper should be interred?'

'Why, where he rests now,' the little man replied. 'Underneath that obelisk, next to the mausoleum. He had pointed out the spot the moment we walked through the gate and he was determined upon it. The others, as I said, had their own ideas, and an argument ensued, at which time Langley calmed the others down, and I was asked to step away for a while.'

'How strange, indeed,' Holmes remarked. 'It could have not been so big an issue, surely?'

'It was to Langley,' Lattimer insisted. 'Even from a distance, I could see he was getting rather warm about it all. At any rate, after another few minutes, he waved me back. "Thank you for your patience, Mr. Lattimer," he told me. Then he looked around at the others as he spoke. "I think you would agree, a fallen comrade should not be shuffled off to a weedy corner, or a dusty spot beside the road. It is our decision that Harry shall rest here with a monument that is befitting to his sacrifice.""

'Given the circumstances, I cannot fault Langley's logic,' I commented. 'What I find strange is that the others, after going to the trouble to bring the lad home, disagreed.'

'Not a one of them said a word,' Lattimer recalled, 'but I could tell by the look on their faces that his remarks had not set well. It was then he requested the obelisk to mark Cooper's grave and a special inscription upon it.

'"A stone that size will have to be brought from Colchester, sir," I told him. "I have nothing close to it in my stock. Of course, there will be an added charge for its transport. For a driver and the wagon."

'"No matter," he told me, "just get it done. And bring the Reverend around tonight so we can discuss details of the service." Again he looked at the others. "This funeral must take place as soon as possible."'

'And their reaction?' Holmes asked.

'There was none. Not a word was said. And so off we went to settle up.'

'You mentioned the inscription was a special one,' I interjected. 'Whatever did it say?'

'It was quite short and to the point,' Lattimer declared. '"To Harry Cooper" it read, "Our Treasured Friend – Bombay". And that was all, save for the dates of his birth and death.' The undertaker sniffed. 'To my mind, it was not much of an epitaph, given the size of that huge stone.'

A thin smile crossed Holmes' face, for what reason I could not imagine.

'Perhaps,' he murmured, demurely, 'but the content is certainly of interest. Ah, well! Thank you, Mr. Lattimer, for your time. This conversation has been most enlightening. You will send my telegram immediately? It is most urgent. I expect a reply within hours, and I wish it to be brought to me at once. You may be assured, I shall defray the runner's expense.'

Holmes reached into his pocket and produced a sovereign, which he placed in the undertaker's hand. Having earlier used the stick, I realised that he was now supplying the carrot.

'Both this message and its reply must remain confidential, you understand? Trust me, at least one life depends upon it.'

Lattimer glanced down at the coin and beamed.

'For twenty shillings, sir,' he insisted, 'my lips are sealed. I'd not even tell my dying mother, if she asked, a minute before her passing.'

'Excellent! Now, where might I secure a carriage for Doctor Watson? He has an engagement to keep with Doctor Blake.'

'Why, I can arrange it immediately,' the little man asserted, clearly pleased at the additional business. He held up the pages of Holmes' telegram. 'But not before I send this, eh?'

Holmes smiled in agreement. 'Send the carriage to the inn, if you would,' he said over his shoulder, as we turned to leave. 'Have the driver ask for Doctor Watson. As for me, I shall be investigating the sites of the previous murders. I should not be hard to find.'

'Yes, sir.'

As we stepped into the street, I again protested to Holmes about keeping my hunting date with Blake – a pleasure, I felt, that should he postponed until another time.

'It seems to me there is much to do,' I observed. 'A visit to Langley's bank in Colchester, perhaps? That would seem a more useful purpose for my carriage.'

'I disagree. Should you make the trip, it would serve no purpose. No official in that institution would divulge a client's financial records to someone off the street. It simply is not done. Should a request come from Whitehall, however...'

'Ah, I see. The addition to your telegram, possibly?'

Holmes nodded.

'You may be assured, Watson, that upon receipt of my telegram, Mycroft faces a busy afternoon. But I feel quite certain that a reply with the pertinent details will be in my hands within a few hours, so extensive are his connections.'

'I have never been quite sure just what his position is,' I admitted.

'He is, most assuredly, a minister without portfolio,' Holmes replied. 'His title would lead you to believe he does little more than audit the books for various Government departments. In fact, he is a policy maker of the highest order, whose opinions are trusted by both the Queen and the Prime Minister alike. In some ways, it would not be inaccurate to say that he is the Government, especially when there is a crisis.'

'And we are in such a crisis, then?' Suddenly, the sunlit afternoon seemed far less fair to me, clouded by the import of our mission.

'We are. You did bring your service revolver, I hope?'

'I did. You specifically requested it.'

'Good. I have my Webley as well. We will most certainly have need of them tonight.'

'You think the killer will strike again that soon?'

'I have no doubt of it. By now, he has heard that we are on his track, and that more constables will arrive upon the morrow. If what I surmise is true, he will have to kill at least once more before the dawn, in order to conceal his murderous scheme.'

'But cannot we not stop him first?'

For a moment, Holmes said nothing. It was, I admit, one of the few times I had seen him look quite so discouraged.

'Much depends on what Mycroft's telegram contains,' he said, finally. 'If my suspicions are correct, then we can act to foil this fiend. I feel confident I have solved the mystery, Watson. But as to the killer's identity ... it remains one in three.'

'One in three?'

'Three soldiers, Watson, who all, at one time, were faithful servants of the Queen.' Holmes slapped his hand in frustration. 'Of one thing I am certain! I need that telegram from Mycroft ... and soon. We have success-fully laid our trap. But if we fail tonight, our killer will most certainly escape. He has been extremely cunning. The evidence, at present, is too thin. We can only hope that we can catch him in the act.

'Otherwise,' my companion added, grimly, 'not even I will be able to bring the man to justice.'

SIX

The home of Doctor Geoffrey Blake was impressive, to say the least. The large gabled structure sat upon the crest of a low grassy hill, sheltered by a stand of stately oaks that partially hid it from the main road below. As my carriage turned in and slowly ascended the long, narrow drive, the grey, imposing front of the house gradually came more into view, sheltered as it was amongst the trees. Thick evergreens crouched beneath the ground floor's wide bay windows, and dark green moss covered the towering walls that rose upwards to its steeply-angled roof of slate. As we drew near, I glimpsed a stone path and wide lawns before the doorway whose threshold was protected by a massive portal of darkened oak as resolute as any Black Watch guard. Rays of sunlight filtered down through the trees, and birds chirped and flitted about from one branch to another. All in all, a more pastoral setting could not be imagined.

I had to admit, as I stepped down from the

trap, that such peaceful surroundings were more than welcome, given the gruesome horrors I had witnessed less than an hour before, coupled with Holmes' grim forebodings. My heart lightened even more, when the front door suddenly swung open and a golden retriever bounded out, followed by Gwendolyn Tate and an older, distinguished-looking fellow in servant's dress.

'Don't worry, Doctor Watson!' the woman called, as the dog barked and raced to my side, his tail wagging furiously. 'Mac is a friendly sort and, according to Geoffrey, he has quite a nose for birds.'

I was, I must admit, engulfed by her charming smile and, as I watched her move gracefully down the path, I could not help but feel envious of my friend's good fortune where the opposite sex was concerned.

'Then he is just what we need for a good afternoon of shooting,' I remarked, as I rubbed the dog's nose and stroked his forehead. 'Where is Geoffrey, by the way?'

'He sends you his apologies,' Miss Tate said. 'He was called to an emergency in the village.' Her face suddenly paled. 'But it had nothing to do with ... well, you know,' she added. 'A boy, he said, had been injured in a fall. By his manner, I took it he would not be long, though he did say he would be visiting Meg Pryor as well.'

'Think nothing of it,' I told her. 'I understand completely. Such matters are all part of a doctor's day.'

'Have you eaten?' she asked. 'I have prepared sandwiches and tea.'

'That would be splendid,' I replied. 'For although hardly over, it has already been quite a trying day thus far.'

'Come inside, then. Parker will collect your bags. Parker, this is Doctor Watson, an old friend of Geoffrey's from the war. He and Mr. Holmes will be staying with us for a few days.'

The old fellow smiled and extended his hand.

'Glad to meet you, sir,' he said. 'And when should we expect Mr. Holmes?'

'I am not certain,' I admitted. 'He told me he had much to do. Late afternoon at the earliest, I should imagine.'

'Very well. I shall keep an eye open. When he does arrive, I shall inquire as to if he, too, requires some refreshment.'

'By then,' Miss Tate chided, 'I would hope our ardent hunters will have returned from the fields with at least a dozen birds, to satisfy our appetites. Even my father, city dweller that he is, often praises my roast partridge.' She gave me a knowing look. 'And, I have no doubt,' she added, 'that you and Geoffrey will be quite famished, after tramping over the countryside.'

As we entered the main hall, I could not help but pause, for it was unlike anything I had seen before. The interior was constructed entirely from stone, with high, spacious archways that opened into the rooms beyond. Impressionist seascapes of high cliffs, boats and sandy beaches hung from the walls, and at the far end of the hall, sunlight poured through a giant, sweeping window that illuminated both the room and the polished oaken stairs that led to the rooms above.

'These walls were originally part of an old Norman castle,' Miss Tate said, noticing my fascination. 'Rather than tear them down, Ferguson incorporated them into the plans when he built here some years ago. I must admit, the large archways do provide a quite open feeling. No adjoining room on this floor is completely closed off from another.'

'I thoroughly agree,' I told her. 'The mood is certainly most relaxing. I think, if I closed my eyes, I could almost smell the salt of the sea breeze, and hear the lapping of the waves upon the shore.'

'Why, Doctor Watson,' she exclaimed, 'I have never heard it put more eloquently! Are you a talented writer, then, as well?'

'I have published accounts of my friend's cases,' I replied, with a smile. 'As to their merit, Holmes and I quite often disagree.'

'You are too modest, I am sure,' she said. 'Come along. I shall have your food brought to you in the study. As a military man like Geoffrey, I think you will find it interesting. I'll direct him to you immediately, when he returns.'

No sooner had I sat at the table, than Parker appeared with a tray of sandwiches and tea, as well as a glass of claret that I found quite to my liking. Knowing I had a rigorous afternoon before me, I dug in heartily. Dinner, I knew, would depend on the whims of Holmes' erratic nature, now that he was clearly on the scent. My odds of actually partaking of Miss Tate's sumptuous partridge, I calculated, were no better than one in three.

So great was my hunger, that within minutes I had devoured several of the tasty sandwiches, and washed them down with gulps of tea and claret. Glancing about the room, and recalling Holmes' instructions, I decided to investigate, and began to walk about with my glass of wine in my hand.

Blake's study was dominated by a huge stone fireplace, with ornate bookshelves inlaid on either side. Before the hearth, a couch, stuffed chairs and a number of small tables had been strategically aligned, so placed, I gathered, so as to catch as much of the fire's heat as possible, during the draughty nights of winter. Above the fireplace, crossed swords and a shiny lancer's helmet hung. I observed a wall display of various swords and knives. Evidently souvenirs from Blake's tour of duty in Afghanistan. An ornate gun case sat nearby containing a row of shiny weapons of various makes and calibre.

Turning round, I strolled to the other side of the room where sunlight streamed in through tall windows that noticeably warmed that half of the chamber. It was there that my good friend's desk was located, along with a large globe and a table that was presently piled high with correspondence, books and magazines.

For the second time that day, I could not help but feel envious of the turn Blake's fortunes had taken. Compared to this, our modest lodgings at Baker Street and the cobbled venues of London seemed very drab, indeed.

It was at that moment, as I consoled myself with another sip of wine, that something I had missed earlier suddenly came to mind. Quickly, I retraced my steps across the room and gazed up, stunned by what I saw.

One of Blake's knives was missing!

Needless to say, I was startled, as Blake burst into the room.

'Watson!' he cried, motioning towards my plate. 'Now that you have staved off the pangs of hunger, I take it you are ready for an afternoon in the countryside.'

'Ready, indeed,' I replied, 'if you can find a weapon to my liking.'

'No problem there,' my friend asserted. Opening the gun case, he brought out a long shotgun with twin barrels. 'Try this on for size.'

Twice, I swung the weapon around, sighting as if to fire.

'Well,' Blake asked, expectantly, 'how does it feel?'

'Frankly, it seems a little heavy,' I told him. 'Due to the added barrel length, I would suggest.'

Blake smiled.

'You are correct. An extra inch and a half,

to be exact. What you have there is a Simpson, hand-crafted by a local gunsmith in Coggeshall. It may be slightly heavier, but it will give you plenty of added range ... a decided advantage when small, quick birds like partridge are your prey.'

'If they are as quick as you describe,' I remarked, 'then I shall take any advantage possible. Gather me some shells, and I shall give this cannon a try.'

'A cannon it may be,' Blake rejoined, 'but I'll wager you have never lifted a gun like that before.'

'No, I cannot say I have,' I admitted, 'but it is an interesting piece.'

'And a rare one. Many local hunters possess them. But outside of Essex, I doubt you would find another dozen in the whole of England.'

'Indeed. Then I look upon this as both a challenge and a privilege.'

Putting down the gun, I strolled over to the fireplace.

'Your study is fascinating,' I told Blake. 'All the trappings of both a military and a professional man ... the crossed swords and helmet are most impressive.'

'The sabres are mine,' Blake said, as he joined me, 'the rest I gathered up and brought back...' He lifted up a rifle that was leaning against the wall. 'This Jezail musket was given to me by a patient, after I managed to save his leg. "Take it as a good luck charm," he said, "and may your luck be as good as mine."'

Blake's words touched me, and brought back a flood of similar memories of my days in the services.

'Why is it,' I asked, 'that they so often consider us Gods when we are only humans?'

'In times so horrible,' Blake replied, 'I think we all must have something to believe in. God sometimes, just doesn't work. In their case, it was us.'

Realising the truth in what he said, I resignedly drained my glass.

'How true,' I concurred. 'And, at times, what a burden it is to carry.'

For a moment, neither of us said a word.

'Regarding this room,' Blake opined, finally to break the silence, 'there is still much to be done.' He pointed to a blank spot on the wall, to the left of the massive hearth. 'That space I am saving for a map of the northern provinces, if and when I can find one of the appropriate size.'

My earlier conversation with Holmes, outside Lattimer's shop, came to mind.

161

'My suggestion would be to ask Sherlock Holmes,' I told him. 'His brother, Mycroft, works closely with the Foreign Office. I feel certain, should we inquire, that such a chart could easily be procured.'

'Do you really think so?' Blake asked eagerly. 'Are you sure Mr. Holmes would not mind?'

'Not at all.'

Turning towards the drinks cabinet, I decided to reveal what I had discovered.

'I must say, your display is quite impressive,' I commented, 'but have you noticed that one of your knives is missing?'

Blake paled noticeably.

'What?!' he cried, rushing past me. 'But that cannot be. I am certain it was here the last time I looked...'

'Indeed. And when would that have been?'

Blake hesitated. 'Why, well, last week, I guess. Before all this...'

'I see. And what kind of weapon was it?' I inquired.

'A tulwar. I picked it up off the road ... after Peshawar.'

'A tulwar,' I remarked, with a shudder. 'What a ghastly weapon, when wielded by uncaring hands upon the helpless. What the natives did to our wounded with those is something I shall never forget.'

'Nor I,' Blake agreed. 'In fact, there is nothing of that Godless side of the world I can recall with any pleasure.'

Grabbing shells from the gun case, Blake handed me the Simpson and took out a standard Purdey for himself. 'Enough of this,' he said, determinedly. 'I shall speak with Parker about the knife when we return. I'll not let it spoil our afternoon.'

Leaving the house with Mac in tow, we crossed the back lawn and struck out through the open countryside beyond, following a meandering trail roughly north and east for almost a quarter mile before we reached a low stone wall. There we paused to load, then spread out and began to cross an uneven pasture, dotted with occasional clumps of gorse. Mac, all business now, eagerly criss-crossed the grassy plain before us, his tail a wagging semaphore in the air.

After ten minutes or so without raising a bird, Blake called a halt, walked over to me and pointed towards a wooded slope off to the left.

'That rise overlooks the cemetery and the church,' he said. 'Langley's house is just the other side. His property borders mine, you see, and is connected by that path we took to get here. My land ends at the rock wall, where we loaded our weapons.'

'So this is his property, then?'

'Yes. But Stephen has always allowed me to hunt in his grounds. And bring along friends like you, if I so choose.'

'How very generous,' I remarked. 'Hello! I think Mac is onto something.'

Looking back now, years later, I recall that autumn afternoon as one of the most enjoyable in my life. Mac proved to be an able tracker, steady at point, and an excellent retriever as well. And although I undershot my first bird with the heavier Simpson, I quickly adjusted, and found to my delight that the piece did indeed give me the range to pull down birds I would have thought were out of reach. As to our quarry, Blake was correct. The small, dark partridges were incredibly quick when they broke from cover. Had I not had the Simpson in hand, I doubt I would have brought down one. For his part, Blake showed himself to be an expert with the standard-length Purdey, only missing twice the entire afternoon. The highlight of my afternoon was a splendid double I managed from a covey that broke from some thick gorse, sheltered in a small hollow.

And yet, throughout that invigorating out-door foray, my enthusiasm was tempered by a concern over Holmes' whereabouts, and what onerous events lay before us, once the sun began to set. What was he up to? Had he received his telegram from London? If so, what information did it contain? What if, on this occasion, his suspicions were not correct? Where did that leave us? Recalling his dire warning, I feared no matter what Mycroft's missive contained, a dreadful night was yet to come.

We arrived back at the house just as the sun was sinking behind the trees, an orange ball whose rays of warmth were rapidly disappearing. Between us, we had brought down eleven of the small, quick birds for the table ... more than enough, Blake insisted, for the half-dozen who would partake. Miss Tate and her companion, a lithe brunette named Alice Reeve, relieved us of our game, and Parker of our weapons and ammunition. After which, we repaired to the study for a drink.

'You appear to be limping,' Blake observed, as we entered the room. 'Is something wrong?'

'Nothing but an old war wound playing up,' I replied. 'I am not used to so much walking in rough terrain.'

'What is your pleasure?' the Doctor asked. 'I can offer either wine or something stronger.'

'I should like a spot of that malt whisky,' I replied. 'You mentioned it on the train.'

Blake poured and we touched glasses.

'Those little fellows were awfully quick,' I admitted. 'Had I not had your Simpson in hand, I doubt I would have scored.'

'Nonsense. You certainly knocked down your share ... and firing a strange weapon at that!'

'Strange, perhaps, but certainly effective. You must give me the name of that gunsmith from Coggeshall. After today, I am considering a purchase.'

Blake seemed pleased at the compliment.

'And the whisky?' he asked.

'It is superb.'

'Excellent! Not to boast, but I feel it is the best single malt I have ever tasted. Another?'

'Just a small one. I feel I shall have much work ahead of me tonight.'

My heel ached as I walked to the window, where I peered out at the growing dusk.

'It will be dark soon,' I remarked. 'I wonder what is keeping Holmes.'

'I have no doubt he will be along soon,'

Blake said, as he handed me my glass. 'I only pray that he has had some success.'

'More than I had dared imagine, Watson!' came a familiar voice.

Instantly, we both span around, startled at the sound of my companion's voice, to find him standing in the room.

'Holmes!' I exclaimed, with some relief. 'I must admit, I am certainly glad to see you. I was beginning to worry.'

'My apologies, Watson,' he replied, 'but I have had an extremely productive afternoon. Suffice to say, Mycroft's reply to my telegram and a brief but enlightening trip to Colchester have provided me with the final pieces to the puzzle...'

'Then you know the identity of the killer?' Blake exclaimed.

Holmes raised a cautioning hand.

'I know only that there are still two men involved,' he stated. 'There is a chance they may be working together. But I am staking all that is not the case.'

'But why not simply arrest them both?' I asked. 'That would seem the best solution to me.'

'Not so. As I mentioned to you earlier, while I have solved the puzzle, I have no positive proof. We must catch him, or them, in the act tonight. If we succeed, all will be well by morning.'

'This is good news,' Blake said. 'Can I help in any way?'

'Thank you, Doctor, no,' Holmes told him. 'The best you can do this night is to remain here, armed and on guard, in case the killer comes your way. You do, after all, have Miss Tate and the others to consider.'

At that moment, we were interrupted by a loud crash and a shout from the outer hall. Running footsteps drew near; then Parker burst into the room, a distraught look upon his face.

'You must come at once!' he cried. 'It is Mr. Langley. He has been injured and is bleeding!'

Rushing into the hall, we found Stephen Langley lying on the stairs. Behind him, the huge front door hung open, and a nearby coat rack had been knocked upon the floor. Rising slowly, Langley groaned as he held his right arm tightly, his broad face grimacing in pain. The sleeve of both his coat and shirt were torn, and blood seeped through the clenched fingers of his left hand. A large bruise could also be seen above his left eye.

'Good Lord!' Blake cried, as he ripped away cloth and began to examine the wound. 'What has happened here?'

'It was the "Ripper",' the other gasped, his eyes wide with terror. 'I was attacked upon the road. Thank God I had a stick and my gun, or the devil would have had me!'

'Parker, bring my bag immediately,' Blake ordered. 'And a pan of hot water, as well. Give me a hand, Watson. We shall remove him to the study.'

In no time at all, Blake had cleaned and stitched the wound to Langley's arm, which clearly had been made by a knife of some derivation. Realising he did not need my assistance, I went to the drinks cabinet, and brought the wounded horseman a glass of brandy.

'You are a lucky man,' Blake told him, as he knotted the final stitch. 'It is a flesh wound, nothing more. Had the knife severed the muscle, you would have had a stiff arm for life.' Carefully, he examined the bruise on Langley's forehead. 'It appears to be a glancing blow, superficial as well,' he concluded. 'I doubt there is any concussion.'

The physician held up two fingers. 'How is your vision?' he asked.

'I can see fine enough,' Langley answered, 'but my head is throbbing like the devil. And

I feel a bit weak at the knees.'

It was at this point Holmes intervened.

'Considering what you have been through, that is quite understandable,' he assured him. 'But if you are able, I should like you to tell us everything you recall of this assault. We are at a critical juncture in this matter, and your observations should help immensely.'

Langley took a sip from his glass.

'I had been in town on business,' he said, 'and because the weather was so fair, I decided to walk the distance, rather than ride. It was a simple matter ... the sale of a gelding to a farmer, sealed by a drink at Weatherby's.' He looked over at Blake. 'On my return, my intent was to enjoy the remains of the day with a brisk walk through the fields. I was just approaching your house, when I was attacked by a creature who rushed out from the woods, growling like a dog as he came at me with a fearful knife in hand. Wildly, I swung at him with my stick ... and I connected well, I think, as I heard a yelp of pain. As I struggled to regain my balance, he came at me again and swung the knife. I felt a shooting pain surge through my arm, and fell. Luckily, as he attempted to strike at me again, I was able to free my revolver and get off a shot. I do not think I hit him, but knowing I was armed must have scared him off, as he turned and ran back into the woods. After that, I lay there for a time. Then knowing your door was close by, I immediately made my way here. Forgive my intrusion, but you have no idea of my relief, when I saw your light.'

'Not to worry,' Blake assured him. 'We are only glad that you are safe.'

Holmes gave the wounded man a piercing look.

'Is there anything else about your attacker you can recall?' he asked, pointedly. 'His features ... height or weight?'

Langley thought a moment.

'No. It was getting dark and everything happened so quickly. I only remember that he was bearded, much taller than I and that he possessed a distinctive smell.'

Holmes put a thoughtful finger to his lips.

'An odour, you say? Pray, describe it as best you can.'

'It was a stagnant smell, I suppose. I'd say one of slime and dampness. Of someone who is unwashed.'

'And who, perhaps, lives on the marsh?' I suggested.

'Why, yes. Now that you say it, that was

the smell exactly. The creature reeked of marsh and mud, and rotting vegetation.' Langley nodded silently to himself, as if making up his mind. 'Yes, a marsh dweller, to be sure,' he added, grimly. 'That has been Inspector Lestrade's theory all along and, after this, I feel him to be correct.'

Holmes brought out his pipe and filled it, then struck a match and sent blue circles of smoke rising towards the ceiling.

'I should like to view the scene of the attack,' he said, directly. 'Might you be so good as to revisit it with me tomorrow? A closer inspection will perhaps shed more light upon the matter. Once Lestrade's re-inforcements arrive, we can perhaps under-take a search.'

The horseman took another sip from his glass.

'But, of course,' he answered wearily. 'I can lead you to the exact spot. It is not far from here and it is not something I shall soon forget.'

'I understand,' Holmes replied. 'As for now, I suggest you return home, and rest as best you can. You have been through a great deal. A good night's sleep will help you regain your strength.'

Langley drained his glass and rose to go,

albeit a little unsteadily.

'Thank you,' he said to Holmes, 'and to you, Blake, for your prompt and able attention. Until morning, then?'

Blake eyed his patient.

'It is my opinion you should stay here tonight,' he insisted. 'Lord knows, we have plenty of room, and Miss Tate is preparing a marvellous dinner. A messenger can be easily sent to Langley Hall, to notify everyone that you are safe.'

'A gracious offer, but after all you have done, I would not think of it,' Langley replied, stiffly.

Blake would not be put off.

'Nonsense,' he said. 'It is the only sensible thing to do. Why, Mr. Holmes has great confidence that we shall catch the "Ripper" by morning.'

Langley seemed taken aback.

'Is that true?' he asked Holmes, pointedly. 'Are you that close, then, to a solution to these brutal crimes?'

'I believe so,' Holmes replied. 'But much depends on what transpires tonight.'

'Then I shall place my confidence in you, and return home to my own bed,' Langley stated, firmly. 'Blake, there is one favour I would ask. Have you a gun I might borrow for the walk back? I seemed to have dropped mine in the scuffle, and lost my stick as well.'

Without hesitation, Blake strode to his desk and drew open a drawer, then another, and another. A puzzled look crossed his face.

'How strange,' he remarked. 'My revolver is not here.'

I glanced at Holmes.

'If so, it is the second weapon that has gone missing,' I told him. 'A tulwar has also disappeared from Blake's collection of knives upon the wall.'

'No matter,' the Doctor said to Langley, with some irritation, as he crossed the room. 'I shall still make certain that you reach home safely.' From the gun case, he drew another Purdey. 'Parker,' he ordered, 'you shall accompany Mr. Langley, armed with this. Should anyone attempt to halt your carriage, shoot to kill.'

'Come, come, Geoffrey,' Langley intervened. 'This is not necessary.'

'Oh, but it is,' the Doctor replied, sternly. 'Be assured, Parker is a very good shot with this weapon. With a crazed killer stalking about, I refuse to tempt fate again.'

'I quite agree,' Holmes declared. 'Given all

that has happened, I think every precaution should be taken.'

Langley frowned with reluctant agreement.

'Very well,' he said, 'I can see you will not be dissuaded. Perhaps it is just as well, for I doubt I could handle the shotgun myself, in any case. But I can handle the reins and hold a lamp along the way, which, if we do find trouble, should provide us with some warning. But I insist that Parker stay the night at Langley Hall. I will not condone him returning through the woods alone.'

'Your suggestion is a wise precaution,' Blake concurred. 'As to your arm, I shall expect you here in the morning. I will want to re-examine those stitches, and check your general condition.' Blake turned to us. 'If you will both excuse me,' he added, 'I shall see them to the door.'

'What do you make of that, Holmes?' I inquired, once the others had left the room. 'It was a close shave for Langley, you must admit.'

Holmes demurred. 'So it would seem,' he replied. 'You mentioned that a knife was missing.'

'Yes,' I said. 'It was hanging with the others on that wall.'

'A tulwar, you said?'

'That is what I was told by Blake.'

'It is a long, curved weapon, as I recall.'

'Precisely. I should say it would be ideal for hacking someone to death. But wait a minute! Are you suggesting Blake...? I cannot believe a medical man of his experience could perpetrate such acts.'

Holmes shrugged.

'Jack the Ripper was also thought by many to be from a medical background,' he said evenly. 'In this instance, however, I doubt that is the case. No, the disappearance of the knife, as well as his revolver, indicates that someone...'

We were interrupted by the appearance of Miss Tate, and her companion, Alice Reeve. Miss Tate appeared quite upset.

'Normally, I would not intrude,' she told us, wringing her hands as she spoke, 'but I have just heard about the attack on Stephen Langley. I must admit to you that, at this moment, I am terrified. I must know. Have you made any progress?'

Holmes smiled, reassuringly.

'You may calm yourself, Miss Tate,' he said, soothingly, 'for I can say most certainly that neither you nor your friend are in any danger. As to the killer, I have set a trap which I am hopeful that, with the help of Lestrade and Newton, we shall soon be able to spring.'

Holmes glanced at his watch. 'And to that end,' he added, 'we must be off immediately. I told them both that we would meet them at precisely six-thirty at your gate.'

'Off?' I exclaimed. 'But what about dinner? Miss Tate has prepared a feast of partridge which I am sure will be superb.'

'My apologies, Miss Tate,' Holmes said, ignoring my protestations, and the crest-fallen look upon my face, 'but matters are coming to a head. If we are to catch this killer, we must be on our way.'

SEVEN

'Where are we off to, then, Mr. Holmes?' Lestrade asked, as we gathered in the darkness at the side of the road.

'To the home of Allen Hastings,' my friend replied. 'Which, if the information Newton supplied is correct, lies approximately a mile away. A small farmhouse on the right, I do believe?'

'You are correct, sir,' Newton told him. 'You think Hastings is the killer, then?'

'Quite the opposite,' Holmes declared. 'I feel he may well be the next intended victim, as he probably knows by now, if word has reached him of Archer's grisly demise. He will, I am sure, be very much upon his guard this night. And we shall be waiting nearby, to ensure his protection.'

'You don't think he would take flight, then?' I asked.

'No, Watson. I guarantee you, there are thousands of reasons for him to stay.'

As I pondered Holmes' cryptic words, Newton posed another question.

'Might he not suspect that we are coming?' the policeman asked.

'I do hope not. For in spite of his situation, it might cause him to panic and flee. Especially given the attack on Langley!'

'The attack on Langley!' Lestrade burst forth. 'Whatever are you talking about, Mr. Holmes? And when did this occur?'

'Not an hour ago,' my companion replied. 'On the road to Doctor Blake's home. Luckily for Langley, the knife missed his vitals, and he was able to get a shot at him before he fled.'

'Langley told us the man was bearded, and smelled heavily of the marsh,' I intervened.

Lestrade smacked his hand with his fist. 'I knew it!' he declared. 'Most certainly one of those marsh inhabitants, after all. Mr. Holmes, I think I shall go back to Lattimer's myself now and send for those reinforcements you mentioned, and if Langley can supply some fellows, well, all the better. Flushing our bird, come morning, will not be an easy task.'

'It is my belief, come morning, that the bird will have already flown,' Holmes replied. 'Better that you accompany us now, to help ensure we trap our man.'

Newton's puzzled countenance, bathed in the pale moonlight, indicated that he also had doubts about Holmes' theories, in spite of my companion's startling revelations earlier in the day.

'It seems to me, you are aware of more facts than we possess,' he stated. 'How can you be certain?'

'From information I received in reply to my telegram to London,' Holmes explained. 'And, from a particularly enlightening conversation with Mr. Thaddeus Compton, Chairman of the Mercantile Bank in Colchester.' My friend gave me an appreciative look. 'Thanks to Mycroft's prompt response, Watson, I was able to follow up on your suggestion. It was why I returned later than I had planned.'

Lestrade began to ask another question, but Holmes cut him short.

'You must understand, there is no time for this,' he said. 'Our advantage at this moment is slight. We must be in position soon. To indulge your curiosity now might well cost friend Hastings his life.'

Lestrade and Newton exchanged a glance, but neither said a word.

'We are in agreement then?' Holmes asked. 'Very well. You are both armed, I hope?'

Lestrade nodded.

Newton patted the pockets of his outer coat. 'That I am, sir,' he said, with confidence. 'Just as you requested. I have, in fact, two revolvers.'

'Good. Then let us be off. I implore you to keep a sharp eye, and a hand upon your weapons. You may need use of them at any instant.'

My heart was pounding and my heel throbbing as well as we trudged on silently along the country road, for almost fifteen minutes, in the moonlight.

'I have to admit, I do feel naked,' I remarked. 'It is a full moon, after all. To my mind, someone on the lookout would easily see us approaching.'

'It is a two-edged sword, Watson,' Holmes replied. 'For once in position, we should have little trouble observing any movement near the house that transpires.'

'For my part,' I rejoined, 'I would be thankful for something to eat. I have walked about all afternoon, and now I am walking still. My heel is sore, and my stomach is fairly growling.'

Holmes looked at me reproachfully.

'That you can think of nothing but food at this moment is beyond my comprehension,' he remarked, with some acidity. 'Does nothing else trouble you, save your digestion?'

'Now that you bring it up, there is one point,' I said, with some indignation. 'What if Hastings does see us approaching the house? Given the situation as you describe it, he might well panic and open fire upon us.'

'Yes,' Holmes said, drily. 'The thought has crossed my mind.'

After another few yards, Holmes signalled us to a halt.

'What do you think, Newton?' he asked. 'Is this not his lane?'

'That it is,' the Constable replied. 'The house is about thirty yards from the road. And there is a barn to the rear, just off to the right.'

We paused behind some trees just off the road to take in the scene. A small stone farmhouse sat quietly in the moonlight. In spite of the cold, no smoke rose from its chimney, and the windows were dark. Off to the right was the barn that Newton had mentioned – an old wooden structure that I could not believe had been used for years, given the sway of its framework, and the missing timbers in its roof.

'We shall stick to the woods upon the right,

and make our way to the back,' Holmes said, in a whisper. 'I want a closer look, before we disperse. Stick to the shadows, remember! Our killer may be close by. And I have no doubt that Hastings is waiting in that darkened house with a loaded gun in his hand.'

Slowly, we made our way through the stand of trees, being careful to avoid fallen branches or clumps of gorse that might, under the weight of a footstep, cause a noise that would reveal our position. Traversing such uneven ground was an ordeal for me, causing my already aching heel to throb even more, but I kept alert and my hand ready upon my revolver. Finally, we reached a point where the shadows of the aged barn concealed us from the house, and emerged into the moonlight.

Following Holmes, we took cover behind a large woodpile, which offered us an unimpaired view of the rear of the farmhouse and the open field behind. All, as best we could tell, was quiet. Light gleamed from the back door window, and from a curtained window next to it as well.

'That is the kitchen,' Newton whispered. 'My guess is that he has sat down to dinner.'

'Lucky fellow,' I murmured, to no one but myself.

'If so,' Holmes replied, with some relief, 'then I doubt he has heard of Archer's demise, or I doubt that a light would be burning. It appears we have arrived in time.'

Holmes motioned us to follow him back behind the barn again.

'Quickly, now,' he said, in a low voice. 'Let us take our places. Lestrade, I would ask that you and Newton retrace your steps, and hide yourself somewhere near Hastings' front door. Should anyone approach, order them to halt and then cry out. Have your revolver drawn and ready! Do not hesitate to shoot! I assure you, this killer most certainly will be armed and desperate. Watson and I shall keep our watch from here, should he choose to advance upon the house from the rear.'

'Good enough,' Lestrade replied. He motioned to Newton. 'We are on our way.'

For nearly half an hour, Holmes and I sat motionless behind the woodpile, watching for any sign of movement from either the house or the field behind. A light breeze rustled through the treetops, but otherwise we heard no sound. The chilly night remained peaceful and serene.

Holmes, I noticed, as the time wore on, was growing increasingly impatient. Some thought had sparked him into restlessness.

'I do not like it, Watson,' he said, finally. 'It is too quiet. We have not heard a sound from the place, nor seen any movement whatsoever.'

'I think it not disturbing. If Hastings has indeed heard of Archer's death, I cannot imagine he would sit in a lighted room. More likely, he would wait armed and ready, in an adjoining, darkened chamber. A lamp or candle in the kitchen might well be a ploy to gain advantage.'

Holmes swung round, a look of revelation on his features, which seemed frozen in the moonlight.

'Or time,' he said. 'Good Lord, Watson, I have an awful feeling things have gone awry. Keep watch, will you? I can only pray that I am not mistaken.'

Without a word, he leapt from our hiding place, and sprinted across the moonlit lawn, his lean frame quickly disappearing into the shadows of the farmhouse. For a moment, I thought I could make out his dark form, crouching next to the wall. Then suddenly, he was gone from sight!

Unnerved, I began to count the seconds, as my eyes searched the dark shadows intensely. To my dismay, Holmes was nowhere to be seen. This was, I decided, no time for caution. Drawing my revolver, I stepped out from the woodpile, and began to advance rapidly upon the house, the moonlight casting my moving shadow before me.

'Watson!'

Hearing Holmes' cry, I instinctively leapt forward, charging towards the sound of his voice. The pain of my heel was forgotten now, as I forced myself to keep moving. Crossing into the shadows, I pointed my revolver at a dark square which loomed before me. An open window!

Cautiously, I edged closer. My grip on my gun tightened.

Do I enter, or wait? I asked myself. The question hammered in my brain, as I tried to decide what was best.

Relief flooded through my body as I heard my good friend's voice.

'It is alright, Watson,' Holmes assured me from the black interior. An instant later, he appeared at the sill, his face a mask of disappointment.

'It is as I feared,' he declared. 'We are too late. The clever devil! He has remained one step ahead and beaten me at my own game.'

'Hastings?' I inquired.

'He is dead. Cut up like the others. His body lies on the kitchen floor.'

At that moment, we heard a shout, followed by a gunshot ... and then another. Immediately, we rushed out towards the gate.

'It must be Lestrade and Newton!' Holmes exclaimed, as we crossed the yard. 'Someone must have come their way!'

To our dismay, we found Lestrade lying upon the road and clutching his left leg with Newton at his side.

'Someone just ran from the house,' Newton stated, as we approached. 'I ordered him to halt but he opened fire...' he paused, '...and Inspector Lestrade went down. I got off a shot as well, but I doubt that I hit him. He was running awfully fast.'

In the moonlight, I could see the deep frustration on my friend's face.

'The scoundrel!' he ejaculated. 'He has beaten us by a whisker, and silenced our last witness.'

Holmes shook his head dejectedly.

'There is no way around it,' he murmured, as if to himself. 'But for my miscalculation, Hastings would still be alive. Given what happened earlier, I never dreamed the killer could possibly arrive before us.'

Try as I might, I could not fathom what Holmes was thinking.

'More importantly.' he said, as if shaking himself from his reverie, 'let's get Lestrade inside.' I could see that my friend, for whatever reasons, was quite disappointed with himself. 'Not that it matters now, but I shall take a quick look around, Watson, while you examine his wound.'

Hoisting Lestrade between us, Newton and I helped him into the deserted house. Upon entering the dimly lit kitchen, I determined that the Inspector's wound would need serious attention. The bullet was still in his thigh, and he had lost a significant amount of blood. Quickly, I fashioned a makeshift tourniquet from a tea-towel and a spoon, then sat him in a chair to rest. That done, I bent down to examine Allen Hastings' lifeless body, which lay sprawled across the kitchen floor. In the pale candlelight, I could see his cotton workshirt was torn and soaked with blood. The cause of death, I concluded immediately, was a vicious knife attack not unlike those which befell the other victims.

'Judging by the condition of the body,' I remarked, 'I would say he has not been dead for long.'

'I would agree,' Holmes said, as he glanced round. He groaned in dismay. 'You will also notice that nothing has been disturbed. No broken dishes, no overturned chairs ... why, the butchery must have been going on while we waited behind the woodpile!'

'Then you must have surprised him when you entered through the window,' I surmised. 'That is what caused him to flee the house, and race off up the lane.'

'He did have time for one thing, though,' Holmes remarked, pointing to an open bottle upon the counter. 'What did I tell you, Watson? A final toast to a former comrade? – Halloa, what is this?!'

Grabbing up the candle, Holmes strode to the far corner of the room. Upon the floor lay a long, bloodstained knife, of Indian derivation which I recognised immediately.

'That is a tulwar,' I declared. 'I would guess it is the one that formerly hung on the wall of Geoffrey Blake's study.'

In spite of his considerable pain, Lestrade immediately drew himself up from his chair and hobbled to our side.

'What is this?' he demanded. 'Why, if that is indeed Blake's weapon, then I think I shall have a little talk with the good Doctor, once this wound is dressed.'

'I would not go far with that line of reasoning,' Holmes advised him. 'For while I have no doubt this is the murder weapon, I can say with all certainty that Blake is not the killer.'

Lestrade gave Holmes a weary look.

'Well, if not?' he asked. 'Who is? Who is this "Chilford Ripper"?'

'The "Chilford Ripper",' Holmes stated, 'is Stephen Langley.'

'Langley!' I exclaimed. 'But that cannot be. He was attacked himself this very night.'

Holmes shook his head.

'No, Watson. It was a ruse, a desperate attempt to avert suspicion, and buy time. Leaving Blake's tulwar here was an attempt to do the same.' Holmes contemplated things briefly. 'At least we have him on the run. Our Scotland Yard story, it seems, has paid dividends.'

'But the man was wounded,' I insisted. 'You saw his arm and forehead.'

'I saw a bruise, and a cut upon his arm, both on his right side. Both could have been easily self-administered, since he is left handed ... as was Stanley Archer's killer.' He smiled as I showed surprise. 'I noted as much when he took your glass of brandy. Well, he certainly cut things close. He must have come here directly, after staging his performance in Blake's entrance hall.'

'But he could not,' I declared. 'He had Parker, armed with a shotgun, at his side.'

'I am afraid,' Holmes replied, pointedly, 'that Parker, like Hastings, is no longer among the living. Langley is, after all, quite strong and would also have had the element of surprise.'

'Good Lord!' I cried. 'What are we to do, then? In spite of all that has happened, we have not one shred of evidence to connect Langley to these crimes.'

'There is only one thing we can do, Watson. We must catch up with him before he flies. And mark my words, unless the devil himself intervenes, he will fly tonight.'

While we were talking, Lestrade, I noted, had returned to his chair, and seemed to be in considerable pain.

'Our first duty,' I insisted, 'must be to secure medical assistance for the Inspector. His wound is serious.'

Holmes turned to the wounded man.

'Time is short,' he told Lestrade, severely, 'and given your condition, I would not expect you to try and render more assistance. What I suggest is that we dispatch Newton back down the road, to fetch Doctor Blake and a carriage. The good Doctor can tend to you while we continue on.'

Painfully, Lestrade nodded his assent.

'I understand your situation perfectly,' he said. 'If you are correct, Langley must not escape. You are off to Langley Hall, then?'

'No,' Holmes replied. 'Our next stop is the graveyard. I can think of no more appropriate place.'

EIGHT

My heel was throbbing, as I struggled to keep pace with Holmes, as we hurried along the moonlit road leading back to town. Try as I might, I could feel my strength was ebbing, given the afternoon's hunt, the sojourn to Hastings' cottage, and now this strenuous march to whatever lay before us.

'My dear Holmes,' I finally asked, 'might we slacken just a little? All this walking today has exhausted me and my heel is hurting terribly.'

To my surprise, Holmes stopped at once. It was not like him, I knew only too well, to show sympathy or emotion when he was on the chase.

'My apologies, Watson,' he said. 'As always, you have been my stalwart companion, a trustworthy friend through thick and thin. The last thing I want is to overwork my sturdy workhorse, for I have no doubt I shall have need of your strength this night. Besides, upon second thought, I feel we can afford to proceed at a more leisurely pace.'

'I do appreciate it,' I admitted, 'but why is that?'

'Because, I imagine, Langley is quite preoccupied at this moment, toiling away at an arduous task that should occupy his energies for a decent time.'

'How so?' I asked, with some surprise.

Holmes smiled at me conspiratorially.

'Because, there is one last thing he must do, before he flees. He must dig up the late Harry Cooper's remains.'

'What?!' I cried, astounded. 'Are you telling me this fiend is not only a brutal killer, but a grave robber as well?'

'I am. For robbery of stupendous consequence is what lies at the heart of this sordid matter.'

'And however did you deduce that?'

'Come, come, old fellow. You are familiar with my methods. It was merely a matter of observation and the information supplied to me by Mycroft's telegram,' Holmes explained. 'It substantiated my theory entirely, like a glove with a perfect fit. When I joined you at Blake's home, the only thing that remained unclear was the identity of the killer. Was it Langley, or was it Hastings?' Holmes shrugged. 'And we now know the answer to that.'

'Then I take it, these four servicemen were involved in some sort of conspiracy overseas?'

'It was a conspiracy of some magnitude, to be sure. So much so, that the Government has kept the whole affair under wraps for years.' Holmes paused a moment, his eyes gleaming with excitement in the moonlight. 'What we have uncovered here, Watson, is the solution to one of the greatest crimes of the decade. Should we bring it to a successful conclusion, it will be cause for a collective, albeit unofficial, sigh of relief, once the news reaches Whitehall.'

While I have never asked, I am certain to this day that at that moment I was the picture of astonishment as I began to understand the enormity of what Holmes was imparting.

'Pray then, tell me what you know of this monumental crime,' I urged, with some exasperation. 'I am quite amazed, I do admit.'

'The details are many, and must wait for later,' my friend replied. 'Suffice to say that Langley and his friends brought an immense fortune back from India, more than enough to supply their needs for life. That they all settled here was no coincidence. After all, how else could they keep an eye upon each other?'

'An unholy alliance, to be sure,' I commented.

'Indeed. The plan, it seems, was to lay low for a time, before they shared their illegal hoard. Langley, I have no doubt, helped the others, with the promise of repayment in the future. What had he to lose? Upon his return, Briarwood was still flourishing, after all.'

Lattimer's words immediately came to mind.

'Until his gambling undid him.' I suggested.

'Precisely. To start with, he sold off his stable's prize assets, in an attempt to cover his losses. And then, he took out loans. In spite of all this, within a few years, his financial position, along with Briarwood's reputation, had been eroded considerably.'

'Then his only means of reversing things was to kill the others and take claim to the entire hoard?'

'Yes.' Holmes smacked his hands in frustration. 'Unfortunately, in spite of my best efforts, he has already accomplished the first, and is currently attempting to do the second.'

'What is his plan, then?'

'To flee to the coast and safety. Mersea most likely. From there, a fast boat could have him in Ramsgate in a few hours and in Calais by morning. Once on the Continent, who knows where he might go? Switzerland? Austria? Anywhere! Given his resources, I deem he would be near impossible to find.'

'Then our only course is to stop him now,' I said, resolutely. 'And I have no doubt we shall. True, this man is ruthless, but he is no Moriarty.'

'Hardly,' Holmes commented, glumly, 'but at the moment, he is succeeding.'

'But only for the moment,' I insisted. 'I have always felt that Moriarty's demise was positive proof that good is meant to triumph over evil. Despite his cunning, time and circumstance caught up with the professor, and I am certain they will catch up with Langley as well.'

'I pray you are right, Watson, for it is all in our hands now. We are the Government's last defence. Ah, there is the village, straight ahead.'

As we made our way along the street, I immediately noticed that Weatherby's hostelry was already closed, its windows dark and doors shut tight.

'That is unusual,' I remarked. 'Although,

perhaps there were few customers tonight, given all that has occurred.'

'It is not only Weatherby's,' Holmes replied. 'Take a look about, Watson. Do you see a soul, or a light shining anywhere? To put it plainly, the people of this village are in hiding. Fear has caused them to bolt their doors this night.'

Moving on, we crossed the square stone bridge. Beneath us, the black, glistening waters of the stream rushed noisily on their way. As we approached the church, Holmes put a hand to my arm, and drew his gun from his coat.

'From this point on, we must be silent,' he warned, in a whisper. 'Have your weapon ready, Watson. With luck, we may surprise him.'

My pulse quickened as we passed beneath the dark, foreboding arch of the cemetery gate. Save for the soft rustle of the breeze among the trees, all was deathly still. Revolver in hand, I steadily followed Holmes' advance, as we crept carefully amongst the pale white rows of headstones in the moonlight. Off to our right, an owl hooted, causing me to start. Regaining my composure, I crept on, watching carefully that I might not stumble on the uneven, grassy ground among the graves.

A few moments later, I silently cursed my luck. My heel had begun to throb again. Determined as I was not to let Holmes down, I ignored the pain and continued onwards.

Ahead of us, I glimpsed what I now felt certain was our destination, the stone mausoleum, and before it, shining malevolently it seemed, the large dark obelisk that marked the spot of Harry Cooper's grave.

Suddenly, Holmes crouched down in the shadow of a large gravestone, and motioned me to join him.

'Look!' he whispered.

Some twenty yards ahead, beside the obelisk, stood a single horse and dray. I shuddered. Protruding from the rear of the wagon, clearly visible in the moonlight, were a pair of human feet!

'Heaven help us!' I gasped. 'The fiend has dug him up already.'

'Quiet!' Holmes whispered, as he began to move forward. 'Carefully now! Our killer is close by.'

Slowly, we moved from one monument to the next, working our way around to the left, away from the obelisk and mausoleum, as we drew closer to the cart. When we were some ten feet away, we knelt again, and for a few agonising seconds, watched and listened for any sign of movement or sound. Strangely, I noted, the ground before the obelisk had not been disturbed.

Motioning me to remain, Holmes rose and quickly stepped up to the cart, looked inside, and signalled me to follow. In the back of the conveyance, lying next to the body, were a pick and two shovels.

'My God!' I exclaimed. 'It is Parker.'

'You are correct, Doctor Watson!'

Jolted by the deep voice behind me, I swung round, in time to see Stephen Langley step from the shadows not far away. His right hand held a revolver, the left the shotgun that Blake had sent along with Parker earlier. Upon his face was a look of devilish satisfaction.

'Throw your guns into the wagon!' he ordered fiercely, as he advanced upon us. 'Try anything and I will shoot you.'

I glanced at Holmes, who signalled that we should obey.

'That's better,' Langley said, once he heard our weapons land inside the cart. 'I am sorry you had to view poor Parker there. Forgive me, but I haven't had time to bury him.' He gave my partner a menacing look. 'Unfortunately, I have had a rather busy evening on your account, Mr. Holmes.'

'You seem to have recovered remarkably from your injuries,' Holmes observed. 'I must commend you. It was a fine performance. But it did not fit the pattern of course. Not late at night, nor against someone alone in their home. Still, you carried it off remarkably well.'

'But not well enough,' the other replied. 'I realised that when you placed that drink into my hand.'

'How better to confirm that you were left-handed?' Holmes remarked. 'The natural inclination, after all, would be to use your dominant arm to inflict a wound upon the other, as well as the scrape upon your brow. You claimed you lost your stick and revolver during the fracas, yet I saw no stains of dirt upon your clothing, which meant you had not been jostled to the ground. If so, it seemed a little far-fetched that you should have lost your gun while standing in the road, watching your attacker flee.'

The big man sneered.

'It seems you are a very clever and observant man, Mr. Holmes,' he said, coldly.

'Crime is common but logic is rare,' Holmes declared. 'Besides, I suspected you long before that.'

'Oh, really. Why?'

'Your attempt to confuse me on where you had served in India was most amateurish. I have yet to meet a serviceman who is not able to recall details of his time abroad almost from day to day. Given Blake's remarks upon the train, and finding Archer dead, I deduced that you and Hastings were the remaining members of a very exclusive club, one that had become much more exclusive in recent days. Thanks to Lattimer, and Mr. Thaddeus Compton, Chairman of the Mercantile Bank...'

'What do you know about that?' Langley snarled.

'Everything. The ruination of Briarwood Stables because of your excessive gambling, the considerable loans you have taken out in recent months. There was, I deduced, but one way for you to square accounts. So by the time you stumbled through Blake's door, I was quite certain you were my man.'

Langley stepped closer, a look of rage upon his wide face.

'You know too much, Mr. Holmes,' he said, menacingly. 'And for that reason, your illustrious career must end now. This is one episode that Doctor Watson will not have the opportunity to chronicle, I am sorry to say.'

'If I were you,' Holmes advised, 'I should be more concerned with saving your own skin. Lestrade and Newton know everything and should be here shortly with constables as well.'

Langley laughed, harshly.

'That is a feeble lie,' he said. 'If either were coming, they would have been with you. I know I hit one of them when I fled Hastings' house. I saw the man go down.'

'It was a superficial wound,' my friend insisted, 'nothing more.'

'It is a chance that I shall take,' Langley replied. Carefully, he stepped over to the cart, where he removed the pick and a shovel and tossed them onto the grass. 'Once dead, you two shall accompany me to the coast, along with poor old Parker. By the time anyone finds you, if they find you, I shall have made my escape.'

Slowly, he levelled the shotgun and revolver at us ... and then, to my immense relief, lowered them once again.

'First, however, there is one last favour which I must ask.'

'And that is?' Holmes inquired.

Langley began to laugh once more, the features of his evil face contorting like some insane mask in the moonlight. He was, I could tell, thoroughly enjoying this moment.

'Since you seem to know so much, I would have thought you would have guessed,' he said to us, in a mocking tone. With the revolver, he motioned towards the cart. 'Grab a pick and shovel, gentlemen, and save me the work. We must dig up poor old Harry before I leave.'

Hate surged through my veins, as I contemplated the fiend's request.

'Not I, sir!' I protested. 'Shoot me, if you must. But I shall not be a part of disinterring a comrade in arms, as part of your ghoulish plans.'

'Your sentiment is admirable, Watson,' Holmes interposed, 'but hardly appropriate. Too many have died for this coffin already. Besides, it will be only a short time before Newton and the others arrive.'

'Still trying that one, eh?' Langley scoffed. 'Well, try all you want ... it makes no difference to me. Off with your coats, now, both of you!'

For the better part of half an hour, we dug steadily, I breaking ground with the pick and Holmes excavating with the shovel. Close by, Langley sat perched upon a gravestone, silently watching us labour in the moonlight. Having relieved us of our weapons, he had decided to put down the heavier shotgun, but kept his revolver at the ready, and pointed in our direction. Deeper and wider the dark hole grew, until Holmes and I stood almost shoulder deep, surrounded by piles of earth all around.

Langley approached and stood above us.

'My, my,' he observed, sarcastically. 'Newton and the others seem to have been delayed. What a pity. They might have helped you. The good Doctor seems a little fatigued.'

Although my heel was throbbing mightily with every swing of the pick, I gave the man a defiant look.

'I am doing quite well, thank you,' I replied, testily.

'No, no, I do insist you rest. There are a few questions I should like to ask your illustrious friend.'

'Such as?' Holmes inquired, as he leaned upon his shovel.

'However did you discover our little scheme? The Government, I was told, had taken great pains to conceal it from the public.'

'My brother Mycroft, who is privy to all that goes on in the Colonial Office, had sought my assistance at the time the theft occurred,' Holmes answered. 'Alas, for political reasons, the Prime Minister decided that my presence in Bombay might cause undo attention at what, for him, was an inappropriate time.'

'But when did you first suspect?'

'It was when Blake recalled to Watson how the four of you had all served in the same regiment in Bombay. Your return here together seemed most irregular, far more than coincidental to me. And then I saw this obelisk, and learned of your insistence on this plot. The implications were crystal clear. What better marker to help you keep an eye on things, yet in a place so secluded from the village? All that remained was to verify your ranks and duties, and that you four were, in fact, stationed in Bombay at the time of the crime. Mycroft's reply to my inquiry confirmed that.'

Holmes managed a thin smile. 'Two supply officers, a carpenter, and a dock guard,' he added. 'It did seem, to me, a very intriguing combination.'

For just an instant, a look of regret appeared on Langley's face.

'You are a most ingenious and resourceful fellow,' he declared. 'I must admit, it will be shame to kill you.'

'Then before you do, will you not indulge me and return the favour?' Holmes asked. 'While I understand the overall picture, there are a few cognisant details that still tickle my curiosity.'

Langley's countenance hardened. He pulled out a watch from his shirt pocket.

'Ask what you please,' he said. 'But make it quick. I have an appointment to keep in Mersea that cannot wait, as I am sure you will understand.'

'The document you recovered from Archer's flat? What was it?'

'We had signed a pact, upon our return, admitting our involvement in the theft. It was an insurance policy, of sorts, that no one would swing alone. Harper's copy was easy to find as he had mentioned once that he kept it in his safe. Old Arch, though, was more clever. I had a devil of a time finding his.' Langley paused. 'Thanks to you,' he added, 'I did not have the time to locate Hastings' paper ... not that it matters now.'

'However did you manage to take him by surprise?' Holmes asked. 'Surely, when he learned of Harper's death, he must have suspected this "Ripper" was merely a hoax ... and that he was next upon your list?'

The horseman chuckled.

'I had anticipated that,' he said. 'That's why I made certain he would not know.'

'How so?'

'By making certain he did not go into the village. At first light, I was at his cottage, where I sent him south to Mersea, to fetch a pair of riding boots I had ordered, and undertake sundry other errands on my behalf. It was an easy deception. I knew Allen would never refuse a guinea in his hand, so I paid him in advance for the favour and off he went. I told him I would return for the boots at dusk.'

'At which time you proposed a toast to celebrate the day?' Holmes suggested.

'Yes. When he turned to the cupboard ... that was when I struck.'

'But in your flight, you were not able to take along the boots,' Holmes reminded him. 'Therefore, they must still remain in Hastings' cottage. What better evidence, I think, to send you to the gallows?'

Langley flinched.

'Do not toy with me, Sherlock Holmes,' the big man warned. 'By my reckoning, you are only inches from the coffin. Antagonise me now, and I shall shoot you both this instant and finish the digging myself.'

'Enlighten me, please, on two other

210

matters,' Holmes replied, coldly, 'and then do what you must. Why was Toby killed? Surely, he had no part in this.'

As Holmes spoke, I began to glance about for some means of foiling our intended killer, but given the hole in which we stood, we were at a decided disadvantage.

'His death was unintentional,' Langley answered. 'The drunken old fool came staggering along, just as I stepped around the corner of Harper's shop. I edged back in the shadows, but he looked my way as he walked past. I had no way of knowing if he recognised me in his drunken stupor, but I could not take the risk.'

'And Molly Brighton? Let me guess. I'll wager she was your mistress but she wanted more. Am I correct?'

Langley sneered.

'More? She wanted everything!' Langley roared. 'Oh, I lusted after her, I admit. She was a comely wench, most pleasurable among the sheets. And so, I fuelled her illusions, to a point. I even gave her money to repair her cottage. But marriage? Ha! Never. Not on your life! Child or no child!'

Never had I seen such an intense look of loathing appear upon my companion's face. For an instant, I thought he might attempt to charge the man, but he held himself in check.

'I was wrong, Langley,' Holmes told him, his voice trembling with fury. 'You are not merely a criminal. You really are a devil, a "Ripper". A creature so monstrous that he would use a woman for his pleasure and then, when it suited him, kill not only her, but her unborn child as well.'

Langley appeared unmoved by Holmes' outburst.

'It is easy for you to say, sir,' he replied, 'but, I tell you, the woman was no innocent. Why, she even threatened to tell all, unless we set a date. Oh, she was a coy one, that's for sure!'

Langley held up his right hand, brandishing an impressive gold ring, which held a red stone of some derivation, atop a band of curling snakes.

'That night, she asked to see this,' he said, 'sweetly as you please, and then slipped it on her finger. "This will do 'til the banns are read," she told me. The haughty little tramp! I knew then I had to kill her, but I was just as coy. "Anything you say, my dear," I replied, and off we went to bed. Once she fell asleep, my pillow put an end to it. And then, the "Chilford Ripper" struck again.'

In spite of our precarious position, I could restrain myself no longer. I only wished that I could somehow strike a telling blow at Langley's repulsive face.

'You blackguard!' I cried. 'You are nothing less than the devil reincarnate. Hell surely holds a special hole for you to reside in.'

Langley edged a little closer to the pit, his dark eyes blazing.

'Provoke me, if you choose, Doctor Watson,' he snarled, 'but it will not do you or your friend any good. You are at my mercy and you have only minutes to live, at most. It will be my pleasure to count each one.'

It was at that instant that Holmes threw all his weight upon his shovel, causing the night air to crackle with a sharp, scraping sound.

'It seems,' he remarked, eyeing Langley carefully, 'that we have found the coffin. Come, Watson, a few hefty swings of your pick should do the job.'

With all my strength, I hurled the pick downward and, as earth flew, I was rewarded by the crash of splintering wood. Quickly, Holmes tossed a few shovels full of earth upwards, then dropped down to his knees.

'You are too late, Langley!' he called out. 'Why, there is nothing here but newspaper! What irony of ironies! One of your victims outwitted you in the end!'

'What!' the big man roared, rushing forward. 'Out of that hole, you swine!'

In a flash, Holmes sprung from the shadow of the grave, swinging his shovel with all his might, catching Langley squarely across the shin. Like an enraged bull, he bellowed out in pain, then dropped his revolver as he fell to the ground, grabbing his injured leg.

'The gun!' Holmes cried. 'Grab it, Watson, quick!'

Frantically, I struggled to pull myself upwards, scrambling across a mound of earth, reaching for the fallen weapon. My hand was but an inch away, when Langley's boot caught me in the side, doubling me over in pain.

Gasping for breath, I saw Holmes rush for the cart where our revolvers lay.

'Not one move, Langley,' he cried, swinging around, a gun in hand. 'Stand fast, I say!'

Too late. With an enraged cry, the big man hurled my discarded pick at Holmes, who got off a shot as it flew by him. Staggering to my feet, I saw Langley retreating through the shadows of the mausoleum. In an instant, Holmes was at my side.

'You are injured,' he declared. 'How badly?'

'A rib, I think. Nothing more. Hurry, Holmes! We must not lose him. I shall retrieve my revolver and follow.'

In a flash, Holmes was gone. Gathering my strength, I hurried to the cart and grabbed my gun. With every breath, my right side burned with a shooting pain.

It was then, as I turned around, that I heard what sounded like the slamming of a door above me, and then a shot.

'Holmes!' I shouted, as I looked up. 'Where are you?'

Suddenly, in the moonlight, I could see them both, Holmes and Langley, grappling in mortal combat atop the roof of the mausoleum. Twenty feet above me, they wrestled fiercely, as Langley attempted to wrest the gun from Holmes' right hand. As I watched in horror, the bigger man pinned Holmes against the wall, pounding his hand against the stone until he was forced to drop his weapon.

Repeatedly, I tried to take aim at the villain, but for naught! They were locked too close together, and my strength was ebbing, my hand a little unsteady. Pain continued to stab through me. I felt nauseous, almost faint.

Holmes struggled furiously, but Langley

was able to get an arm beneath him, and with his superior strength, began to lift my friend above him, clearly intent on hurling him over the edge.

'Now I have you, Sherlock Holmes!' Langley cried. 'Your meddling is at an end!'

It was, at that instant, I saw Holmes' right arm slash out, delivering a savage blow to Langley's throat that caused him to lose his hold as he screamed in pain. Dropping my friend, the big man staggered, then turned to reach for Holmes again.

Knowing this was my chance, I fired twice at the dark form of Langley's broad back. As he cried out, Holmes leaped up and gave-the man a mighty shove which propelled him over the ledge and out into the moonlight. Like a large boulder, he hurtled downward, landing upon the upward point of the obelisk with a sickening thud, and a death cry that chilled my bones.

My first thoughts were for my friend.

'Holmes!' I called. 'Are you alright?'

'Thanks to you, Watson,' he answered. 'I shall join you in a moment.'

Slowly, I staggered forward to where Langley lay at the base of the obelisk, his body twisted in an unnatural way His eyes were glazed in death, and his mouth hung open in a garish grimace of agony. A quick examination confirmed my suspicions ... in addition to my gunshot wounds, the fall upon the obelisk had snapped his spine.

A moment later, Holmes was at my side.

'Is he dead?' he asked.

'Yes.' I said, with measured breaths. 'You pushed him but it was the obelisk, his own creation, that broke his back and finally killed him.'

Holmes put a hand upon my shoulder.

'Then it was as you predicted, Watson,' he told me, softly. 'Time and circumstance, my good fellow. Time and circumstance. Step over here a moment, will you?'

I followed my friend to Harry Cooper's grave which we had unearthed so shortly before. To my surprise, Holmes dropped down into the hole once more, and as I watched, began to pry open some of the shattered boards.

In spite of all that had transpired, I was aghast.

'Holmes,' I inquired, 'is this really necessary?'

'It is. I shall now show you, Watson, why your suffering this night has been in such a good cause.'

Without another word, he began ripping

up the coffin's boards. I was astounded, as moonlight flooded its interior.

From head to foot, the entire box was filled with money! More five pound notes than I had ever witnessed.

'Good Lord!' I declared, incredulous. 'Whatever have we discovered here?'

'Fifty thousand pounds, unless I miss my guess,' Holmes replied. 'A trove known only to a few select Government officials as "the missing Wilkinson treasure." As I said, their relief will be immense, when they hear of this.'

NINE

By midnight, things seemed to be well in hand. The industrious undertaker Lattimer had been duly roused from his bed by one of Newton's constables, with orders to procure the bodies of Hastings, Parker, and Langley for interment. While at his shop, Holmes had sent an urgent telegram to Mycroft, informing him of the treasure's recovery, which, thanks to the kindness of the local clergyman, now lay securely under lock and key in the basement of the church.

As to my injuries, Blake's prognosis concurred with mine. Langley's savage blow had indeed cracked the third rib of my right side, and severely bruised the one below it. After treating to me, we rejoined the others – Holmes, Lestrade, Newton, Miss Tate and her companion – in the comfort of Blake's study. A crackling fire warmed the room, and to my delight, Miss Tate had prepared a delicious partridge pie for our late evening repast. Once I was seated, Blake brought me a much-appreciated glass of brandy.

'Thank you, old friend,' I told him, after taking a sip. 'I am somewhat weary. I must admit. After all, it is not every night one is forced to dig a grave ... and narrowly miss occupying it!'

While I partook of the steaming pie, Holmes related the details of our near-fatal visit to the cemetery, after which he drew out a revolver from his coat pocket and handed it to Blake.

'This was in Stephen Langley's hand, when he surprised us,' Holmes explained. 'When I retrieved it, I noticed your initials on the butt.'

'So it was he who stole my knife and gun,' Blake reflected.

'But, of course,' Holmes explained. 'It was his plan to implicate you all along. And it was a clever scenario, indeed, had he been able to carry it out. A number of grisly murders are committed. The weapon used, it is later discovered, belongs to you. You who, at the appropriate time, suddenly vanish, abandoning his practice, home, and fiancée.'

'Then he...'

'...intended to kill you, I have no doubt. My belief is that he had some sort of incriminating scheme in mind for your revolver as well.'

'But who would believe such a story?' Blake insisted. 'After all, what would have been my motive?'

'That we can only speculate,' Holmes said, 'but I suspect, at the proper moment, he would have revealed that you harboured a secret so dark it threatened to ruin you. That Molly Brighton was carrying your child.'

'But what about the others? Harper, Archer and Hastings?'

Holmes shrugged.

'Perhaps they knew. Perhaps blackmail had been threatened. Who knows? The fact is, whatever tale Langley chose to tell would certainly have been hard to refute, since you would not be around to do so.'

'But it is preposterous!' the Doctor expostulated. 'It was I who travelled to London, to specifically secure your aid.'

'And that, my good Doctor,' Holmes assured him, 'was where his plot began to fall apart. It was your act that upset his machinations, forcing him to forgo his original plans to incriminate you. Our presence here made killing you nigh impossible. So he decided to quickly dispose of Archer and Hastings and flee.'

'And when did you first suspect him?'

Blake asked.

'Your comments on the train started my mind racing,' Holmes explained. 'Four soldiers, all of the same regiment, who return here together. And then, when we arrived, I find two of the four are dead. No. If the date of their discharge was as I suspected, it could not be mere coincidence. That is why I telegraphed Mycroft immediately for particulars.'

'Pardon me, Mr. Holmes,' Lestrade interposed, likewise seated with a glass of brandy in hand, 'but there's one thing I would like to know. Why could we not have arrested Langley sooner?'

'On what evidence?' Holmes speculated. 'For all my conjecture, we had not one shred of evidence connecting him to the crimes.'

Lestrade took a sip from his glass. His leg, I could tell, was bothering him more than he chose to admit.

'So tell us, then,' he said, 'what is the real story behind this dreadful business? Where on earth did all that money come from?'

'From the vaults of Her Majesty's Government,' Holmes explained. 'More specifically, from the hold of the British merchantman *Pretoria*, while she was docked in the harbour at Bombay on the night of 22nd August, 1891.' My friend looked about the room. 'But before I speak further, I must foreswear you all to secrecy,' he added, gravely, 'for this is a matter that, if the details come to light, could still cause our former Prime Minister immense political harm. His enemies, I daresay, would receive the news with glee. And while I have disagreed with Mr. Gladstone on more than one occasion, I still cannot bring myself to do that august statesman such a disservice.'

Sombrely, we all nodded our assent.

'Upon that point, I am certain we are in agreement,' Blake told my friend. 'Pray, please continue. I know that I shall not be content, until I possess the reason for these sordid happenings.'

Holmes took a cigarette and lit it.

'Shortly after the Prime Minister took office,' he began, 'he received a confidential cable from Viceroy Adam-Brooke in Bombay, informing him that radical elements of the Indian National Congress were pressing a certain prince from a northern province to join in their efforts to overthrow the British. What they planned, with some aid from the mercenary Afghani border tribes, was nothing short of a mutiny. When the prince had spurned their initial entreaties, threats upon his and his family's lives had followed. While still loyal to Her Majesty, he asked the Viceroy for additional guns and munitions for his troops and funds to buy off the wretched Afghanis.'

'It seems to me,' I interjected, 'that Gladstone had no choice. The whole frontier, as I recall, was at that time a powder keg.'

Holmes paused momentarily, before continuing, but I could tell by the distasteful look on his face that he disagreed.

'Mycroft advised that British troops should be sent in immediately, both to hunt down the radicals and disperse the Afghanis. Otherwise, he reasoned, it would not be long before additional demands were made.

'Gladstone, however, was no Disraeli. He had, ten years before, pulled British troops out of Afghanistan, and now, when faced with a crisis once again, his liberal resolve dissolved as quickly as the sand before the sea. His beloved Home Rule Bill for Ireland was about to come before the House, so he decided to buy time to protect the political *status quo*. A large shipment of arms and a sum of £50,000 was secretly loaded aboard the *Pretoria* and dispatched *post-haste* to Bombay. Upon the ship's arrival, Colonel

Wilkinson, the garrison commander, was to deliver both to the threatened prince.

'On the afternoon of 22nd August, the *Pretoria* docked in Bombay as scheduled, supposedly with fresh supplies for the garrison. Wilkinson, as you would expect, came aboard and ordered the ship to be put under heavy guard until morning when unloading of the secret cargo was to begin.

'That night, however, the money was stolen. Gone without a whisper in the darkness. Wilkinson was found stabbed to death in his cabin, and four guards had been likewise killed at their posts. Next to the colonel's body lay a note from the Indian radicals, boasting that the money would now buy weapons for them, insuring the eventual overthrow of English rule.'

'That is an event, I am pleased to say, which still has not occurred,' I remarked, taking another sip from my glass. 'Nor, I trust, shall it ever. Our presence there is the only means I see for stabilising that abysmal region. Left to their own devices...'

Not wishing to say more, I merely shook my head in disgust.

'During the ensuing weeks,' Holmes continued, 'intense and repeated searches were conducted to try and retrieve the money.

No less than one hundred suspects were arrested and questioned. The money, however, was never found.'

'And the guns?' Newton queried.

'The guns were delivered, with appropriate apologies, to the prince. But, ironically, when he learned there were no funds, he accused the British of bad faith and threw in his lot with the radicals instead. Sadly, he remains anti-British and a constant source of worry to this day.'

Holmes threw up his hands in despair.

'As you can see,' he concluded, 'it was quite the diplomatic fiasco, and could not have come at a more inopportune time for the Prime Minister.'

He inhaled his cigarette and then continued.

'Gladstone, who had ignored Mycroft's advice, naturally ordered the whole affair to be hushed up and denied his request that I should go to Bombay and put things right. What he feared, of course, was a scandal that might scupper his precious Home Rule Bill.'

'And which,' I added, 'was later soundly defeated by the House of Lords, as well it should.'

This time, Holmes nodded in agreement.

'That all Gladstone's efforts came to naught is perhaps the most ironic part,' my friend remarked. 'Who knows, Watson? I have always felt, had I been sent immediately to Bombay, I might have uncovered what really took place. It is hindsight, of course. The end of it is that the Prime Minister chose not to take the risk.'

'There is one fact I'd like you to explain,' Lestrade commented. 'However did Langley and his friends steal the money? How did they get it off the ship?'

An amused smile appeared upon Holmes' lips.

'That was the beauty of their plan,' he told the wounded policeman. 'I am convinced that they never did.'

Lestrade's surprise was such that I felt he might drop his glass.

'But if they did not take it off,' he cried, 'why was it not discovered? You state that intensive searches were conducted.'

'Yes. Throughout the city, the surrounding villages and countryside. Indian rebels were what the troops were looking for, after all. What better place, then, to hide the hoard than in the safety of the *Pretoria's* own hold?'

'But surely, the ship itself would have been searched?'

'I have no doubt it was,' Holmes concurred. 'And, given Wilkinson's death, the search was most likely conducted by his second-in-command, Stephen Langley.' Holmes took a long draw at his cigarette. 'Given Langley's rank and duties, it is not too much to suppose that Wilkinson had shared his confidence about the valuable cargo that was soon to arrive.'

'Wait a moment!' I ventured. 'Might not Wilkinson himself have been an accomplice in the theft? A partner who Langley dealt out at the first opportunity?'

Holmes reflected.

'It is a possibility, Watson,' he concluded, 'but since the principals involved in the crime are now all deceased it will be impossible to verify.

'What is certain is that, upon the night of 22nd August, Langley and his three cohorts were aboard the ship. I suspect they first murdered the guards, then Langley visited Wilkinson's cabin on some pretext, killed him, and left the tell-tale note designed to throw the authorities off the scent.'

'But how did they get onto the ship in the first place?' Newton asked. 'A military vessel is always heavily protected and there would have been no reason for their visit.'

'Access was provided by a dock guard named Allen Hastings,' Holmes replied, 'who Langley, I am sure, conveniently assigned to that specific watch some days before. While Hastings provided cover, the others brought aboard a coffin, specially built and weighted by one of the garrison's carpenters.'

'Thomas Harper!' Blake exclaimed. 'Why, of course. It must have been him.'

'The box, filled with bags of sand to give it the proper weight, had probably been hidden nearby days before,' Holmes conjectured. 'It would have been a simple thing for Langley to add it to the *Pretoria's* return bill of lading. After killing Wilkinson and the others, the money was most likely transferred from a strongbox to the coffin, which was then stored in a place deep inside the hold, where it would not easily be noticed.'

'And what was Archer's part in all of this?' Blake asked.

'A very important one,' Sherlock Holmes replied. 'Langley could not have carried it off without him. As Supply Clerk, it was he who drew up a false death certificate, which was then co-signed by he and Langley. Thus, when the *Pretoria* weighed anchor for England some days later, the money was safely aboard, in the guise of the deceased,

Harry Cooper, who had given his life for the Crown.'

Holmes clapped his hands together, an excited look on his lean face.

'You must admit, it was an absolutely daring plan!' he declared. 'While our troops were searching vainly amidst the dusty mountains and valleys for rebel thieves, the stolen money was making its way back across the waves, under guard of the British Government, no less.'

'And once the ship reached England, who signed for it there?' Lestrade inquired. 'And to whom was the coffin delivered?'

Holmes shook his head.

'As to that, I can only speculate,' he admitted. 'However, I imagine Mycroft will have that information, and someone in hand, by dawn. Who knows? It may have been a female confidante of Langley's, posing as a sister to claim her kin? My guess, however, is that it was a friend of Harper's, who transported the box to his shop in Bristol, where it sat untouched until they all returned home some weeks later to claim their prize.'

'But why come here?' Blake demanded. 'Why did they not simply divide the money amongst themselves in Bristol, once they had the coffin in their hands?'

'Two reasons immediately come to mind,' my friend answered. 'First, the trail was still too warm. If any of them had begun spending their share too freely, it most certainly would have attracted attention, and perhaps arrest. And each, remember, possessed a copy of the document they had signed. Hang one and all would hang together.'

'And the other reason?' I inquired.

'Hastings' inclination for the bottle,' Holmes said, extinguishing his cigarette, 'the looseness of a drunken tongue.'

'And so,' I concluded, 'Langley convinced the others to bring the money here, to an obscure village in Essex, where it could remain safely hidden until the time was right to effect the split. Naturally, once here, they had to stay on if only to ensure they received their fair share.'

'Precisely.'

'But why did he suddenly decide to kill the others?' Blake inquired. 'He did not need the money, surely?'

'Oh, but he did. As Lattimer pointed out, Langley's penchant for gambling, and losing, had plunged Briarwood into dire financial straits. Selling off his best horses only bought him time, and he was forced to obtain sizeable loans to stay afloat, using the stables as a guarantee.' Holmes gave us a knowing look. 'Thanks to a Government request, the details of the transactions were given to me this very afternoon in Colchester, by the Chairman of Langley's bank.

'It was then,' he continued, 'that he decided to take the money for himself, and frame Doctor Blake in the process. As in Bombay, he conceived a clever diversion to mask his crime ... the so-called "Ripper" who butchered people in their beds.'

'But why Toby Turner?' Newton questioned. 'And Molly Brighton?'

'Langley suspected Turner had seen him rounding the corner of Harper's store. As to Molly...' my friend sighed '...she was carrying his child and tried to force him into marriage.'

Upon hearing Holmes' words, Miss Tate rose to her feet, a look of shock upon her face.

'That I cannot believe!' she cried out, vehemently. 'Why, Molly would never...'

Holmes sighed.

'It has been said, Miss Tate,' he told her, evenly, 'that the truth at times cuts deeply. But still, the truth it is. An examination would confirm her condition, but I think there is no need. Langley himself admitted the affair to us this very night, and that he was indeed the father.'

Tears welled in the young woman's eyes. Her companion moved to her side, and put an arm about her shoulders in comfort as she sank back into her chair. Blake was immediately at her side as well, and took her hand.

'Dear Gwen,' he said, 'this is a very convoluted matter. It has brought out many things about us here that we did not know. But Mr. Holmes is right. While the truth brings pain, it also brings relief. Oh, we shall grieve, most certainly, for a time, and then, as God meant it, get on with our lives again.'

The Doctor patted his fiancée's arm with affection, which she returned with a look of equal measure. With a heavy sigh, she rose to her feet.

'I think I shall retire,' she said, wearily. 'It has been a long and arduous day. One of many.'

'Ah, but Miss Tate,' Holmes intervened, with some emotion, 'do take heart! For it is, most certainly, the last.'

Silently, she nodded, and walked slowly off into the outer hall.

For a moment, not a word was said as the

two women left the room. It was clear, I felt, that all of us shared Miss Tate's deep sadness, not only for the loss of her dear friend, but for the distasteful circumstances surrounding it.

It was Lestrade who finally broke the silence, as he rose slowly from his chair, using a nearby table for support.

'The hour is late,' he declared, 'so if you will excuse me, gentlemen, I shall return to the inn. I think a bit of rest is in order.' Reaching out, he shook Blake's hand. 'My thanks to you,' he added, 'for your prompt and able attention. I shall, as you requested, keep my leg rested and visit you again in the morning.'

To my surprise, the policeman turned to Holmes and put out his hand to my friend as well.

'I must admit,' he stated, 'that I am in your debt, Mr. Holmes. You have been of considerable assistance in this matter.'

'You have performed nothing less than a remarkable piece of deduction,' Newton interjected, giving Lestrade a chastened look, as Holmes replied with a slight bow. 'To you and Doctor Watson, I am also deeply indebted.' The man paused, rubbing his chin thoughtfully. 'You were right about one thing, sir. The man was devilishly clever in covering his tracks.'

'I would agree,' Holmes declared, 'but thankfully now, it does not matter. Fate has already done for him what he deserves.' With a knowing look, he glanced my way before continuing. 'Time and circumstance have proven our case. Eh, Watson?'

With a weary smile, I nodded in agreement.

'That said,' Newton stated, 'I shall take my leave as well.' He turned to Lestrade. 'Come along, Inspector. If you have room for another, I shall accompany you back to town.'

Once the two policemen had left, Blake refreshed our glasses, and we all took a seat close to the fire.

'Poor Molly,' the physician said, with a faraway look in his eyes. 'Surely, that is the saddest part of all of this. In spite of her weakness, she did not deserve such a fate.'

'Weakness?' Holmes questioned. 'Is that what it is to want better for your life, and for your child? No, I would rather say it was a strength.'

Holmes took a sip from his glass, then uttered an oath and clenched his fist angrily in the light of the crackling flame.

'May he rest forever in the lowest regions

for that abominable act!' he declared, fervently, 'for it was far more than deceit or murder. It was the death of her unborn. Killing the future, which is all we have, when all is said and done. Unfortunately, for all my powers, it was the one thing I could not rectify.'

In the flickering light, Blake and I exchanged a look of sadness. Holmes was right. As physicians, we had both brought many into the world. That, in this case, such promise should be denied was disheartening, to say the least.

Holmes' voice startled us from our thoughts.

'Blake, I have a favour to ask,' he said, solemnly.

'For all that you have done,' the other replied, 'it would be my pleasure, if it is within my power.'

'Each spring, when the flowers about her cottage first appear, would you place a basket upon Molly Brighton's grave? Poor thing. She only wanted better for herself and her child. Fate, it seems to me, has treated her quite cruelly. I can only hope, wherever she is now, that she somehow knows that it was her death that assured this fiendish killer would be brought to justice.'

The following morning, although still weary from our efforts, we managed to rise and make Colchester in good time to board an early train to London. Once seated in our compartment, Holmes lit a pipe and immersed himself, as always, in the dailies, until I interrupted him with a thought that was on my mind.

'Regardless of our political convictions,' I ventured, 'should we not somehow make certain that Gladstone is held accountable for all this? It has been a horrible affair, and I am having some second thoughts, I must admit.'

'For my part,' Holmes replied, 'I feel it would serve no useful purpose, now that he has left office. What good, after all, is there to useless scandal? The mystery has been solved, the criminals punished, and all the money has been recovered. I think that is all we can ask.'

'Perhaps you are right. But there is one further thing, upon reflection, that troubles me.'

'And what is that?'

'Langley said he had lusted long after Molly Brighton. Do you suppose he had a hand in her husband's death, upon the sea?'

My friend reflected for a moment, sending

a blue cloud of smoke swirling overhead.

'It is a thought that cannot be discounted, Watson,' he said, finally. 'Jealousy, after all, was the reason that Cain slayed his brother Abel, so long ago, and that merely over the worth of their possessions. Is it too much, then, to suppose that a man might slay his friend because he coveted his wife? I think not. For if there is one truth that I have learned, Watson, it is that while time moves on, man's motives never change.'

This Large Print Book, for people
who cannot read normal print,
is published under the auspices of

THE ULVERSCROFT FOUNDATION